FRIENDS

STORIES ABOUT

NEW FRIENDS,

OLD FRIENDS,

AND UNEXPECTEDLY

TRUE FRIENDS

FRIENDS

STORIES ABOUT

NEW FRIENDS,

OLD FRIENDS,

AND UNEXPECTEDLY

TRUE FRIENDS

Edited by Ann M. Martin and David Levithan

SCHOLASTIC INC.

NEW YORK TORONTO LONDON AUCKLAND SYDNEY
MEXICO CITY NEW DELHI HONG KONG BUENOS AIRES

The contributing authors and editors have forgone payment of all advances and royalties in order for those proceeds to go to the Lisa Libraries, a nonprofit organization that donates new children's books and small libraries to organizations serving needy children. The purchase of this book is not tax-deductible. For more information about the Lisa Libraries, please visit: www.lisalibraries.org.

No part of this publication may be reproduced, stored in a retrieval system, or transmitted in any form or by any means, electronic, mechanical, photocopying, recording, or otherwise, without written permission of the publisher. For information regarding permission, write to Scholastic Inc., Attention: Permissions Department, 557 Broadway, New York, NY 10012.

ISBN 0-439-83741-3

"The Friend Who Changed My Life" Copyright © 2005 by Pam Muñoz Ryan
"My Best Friend" Copyright © 2005 by Jennifer L. Holm
"Connie Hunter Williams, Psychic Teacher" Copyright © 2005 by Meg Cabot
"Squirrel" Copyright © 2005 by Ann M. Martin
"Smoking Lessons" Copyright © 2005 by Patricia McCormick
"Shashikala: A Brief History of Love and Khadi"
Copyright © 2005 by Tanuja Desai Hidier
"The Wild Prince" Copyright © 2005 by Brian Selznick
"Flit" Copyright © 2005 by Patrick Jennings
"The Justice League" Copyright © 2005 by David Levithan
"Minka and Meanie" Copyright © 2005 by Rachel Cohn
"Doll" Copyright © 2005 by Virginia Euwer Wolff

All rights reserved. Published by Scholastic Inc.
SCHOLASTIC and associated logos are trademarks
and/or registered trademarks of Scholastic Inc.

12 11 10 9 8 7 6 5 4 3 2 1   5 6 7 8 9 10/0

Printed in the U.S.A.   23

First Scholastic Book Club printing, October 2005

The text was set in Adobe Garamond.
Book design by Elizabeth B. Parisi

CONTENTS

THE FRIEND WHO CHANGED MY LIFE
by Pam Muñoz Ryan

I HATED BEING THE NEW KID AT SCHOOL. I was in the fifth grade and my family had moved to a new neighborhood. Already with a size 9 shoe, my feet were an awkward atrocity. My curly brown hair, the result of the religious use of pink rubber curlers, stayed wholesomely off my face with hair clips. How was I to know that straight ponytails and short, blunt bangs were the rage at this school? Since I hadn't yet adopted the no-socks look, my sense of style didn't mesh, either. I wanted to fit in, but I didn't have the all-necessary confidence. To escape, I walked around with my nose in a book. Unfortunately, I wore my vulnerability like a brand-new pair of milk-white Keds — all too ready to be scuffed. A bully took advantage.

Her name was Theresa. She was tiny, wiry, and loud, with blond bangs and the mandatory tightly-pulled-back ponytail. I swore she walked with a deliberate swagger just to get her ponytail to swing back and forth. For a reason unknown to me, she decided that I was worthy of her undivided attention, and every day she waltzed up to me and kicked me in the shins or the back of the legs. I could expect a wallop any time I was off guard, while I was standing in line to go to class after a recess, on my way out of the girls' bathroom, or as I pushed my lunch tray along the counter in front of the cafeteria ladies. *Bam!* Theresa was smart and quick. No teacher ever saw her, and my legs were black, blue, purple, and green within a week.

My mom noticed the marks, but I pacified her by saying that I played on the jungle gym at recess and had bruised them on the bars. I could tell from my mom's expression that she was suspicious of my story. She made me promise I'd play somewhere else. I knew that if I kept coming home with mottled legs one of my parents would eventually go to my teacher. I could only imagine the price I'd have to pay among the other kids if I was seen as both the new kid *and* a crybaby tattletale.

I used to lie in bed every night dreading school and trying to figure out complicated routes to walk from one place to another so Theresa couldn't get to me easily. I had a convoluted method of getting to my classroom, which involved walking outside the fenced school yard and entering the grounds at the opposite end of the campus, then working my way through the kindergarten playground. At recess and lunch I stayed in the open spaces on the grassy field because if I saw Theresa coming, I could at least run.

One day, Theresa chased me on the playground, about to close in with yet another successful attack. Frantically, I ran away from her, glancing back every few seconds to see where she was. I looked to one side and was relieved when I didn't see her. Thinking she had given up, I stopped abruptly and turned around, unaware that Theresa had been running full-speed toward me from the other side. She didn't expect my sudden stop and collided into me and bounced toward the ground. A group of kids standing nearby laughed. Angry, Theresa got up and began kicking me with a fury, over and over. A scrape on my knee reopened and blood trickled down my leg. As much as I wanted to, I didn't cry. I just stood there and took it.

Mary Lou, also in the fifth grade, was the tallest and biggest girl in the entire school, including the sixth graders. She wasn't fat but was sturdy and big-boned and strong. Her red hair, thousands of freckles, and fair skin gave her a gentle giant appearance. Still, no one ever messed with her. When Mary Lou shoved her way through the crowd of kids and took my elbow, everyone backed away, including Theresa.

Mary Lou ushered me to the girls' bathroom. As I stood there, shaking, she took a wad of paper towels, wet them, handed them to me, and pointed to my bloodied leg.

"So, Theresa's been bothering you."

I nodded, hoping that the next words out of Mary Lou's mouth would be, *Well, I'm going to take care of her for you.* I had visions of having a personal hero to protect me — fantasies of Mary Lou escorting me around the school with a protective arm over my shoulder, clobbering anyone who came near me.

Instead Mary Lou said, "You can't let her keep doing this to you. She's never going to stop unless you make her stop. Get it?"

I didn't really get it, but I nodded.

"Listen, she's a pain. But if you don't stick up for yourself, things will get worse. You know that, don't you?"

How could it get worse? I was already paralyzed with fear and had turned into a whipping post for some girl who was half my size. Besides, what did Mary Lou mean about sticking up for myself? Did she want me to *fight* Theresa? That idea terrified me more than being kicked every day.

"I'm not kidding," said Mary Lou. "And if you don't

do something, I'm going to start hitting you, too. Understand?" She made a fist and held it in front of my face.

I thought about Mary Lou's size and weight and gulped. Things could *definitely* get worse. "Yes," I whispered.

"Okay then, get back out there."

Now? Did she mean stand up for myself right now?

I walked back to the playground with Mary Lou smugly following behind. I couldn't see a way out of the situation. In front of me was Theresa and in back of me was Mary Lou. The first bell rang and kids began to assemble in their assigned lines on the blacktop in front of the classrooms. In a few minutes, the second bell would ring and teachers would walk out and get their students for class. The yard duty teacher was out on the grassy field blowing her whistle and rounding up the stragglers. As usual, no teachers would be around to witness my destruction.

Theresa stood in a huddle of girls. Mary Lou nudged me toward her. I had never started a fight before in my life. I had never hit anyone and didn't have an inkling of what to do. My insides shook worse than my outsides. When Theresa saw me approaching, she set her mouth in a grim line, marched toward me, and swung her leg back to haul off and kick me. I jumped back to avoid the kick. I made a fist and flailed my arm wildly, in some sort of ridiculous motion. *Pop!* In a miraculous blow, I caught Theresa in the nose and blood sprayed across her clothes. I don't know which of us was more surprised.

I don't remember what happened next. I know we brawled on the blacktop. Gritty sand scraped the bare skin on my arms. (I would notice the burns later.) As we rolled over and over, tiny pebbles embedded in my face. One of them made a substantial puncture that didn't heal for weeks. (The pock remained for years.) I'm not sure who separated us and broke it up. In a matter of minutes, someone retrieved the yard duty teacher, and she corralled and ceremoniously walked us to the principal's office. I, the nice girl, the good girl, was going to the principal's office for fighting. Devastated, I hung my head.

Sitting on the bench outside the principal's office and waiting to be called in, I worried about several things. Would the school tell my parents? What would my punishment be? What would Theresa do to get back at me? What would the other kids think? Branded, I was now a bad girl.

The yard duty teacher deposited us in two chairs, side by side, in the principal's office and placed the referral slip on his desk. Our principal was a balding man, with glasses and a kind, grandfatherly face. He seemed happy to see us.

Smiling, he said, "Well, girls, I want you to put your heads together and decide what your punishment should be while I make a phone call."

He picked up the phone, and as he made his call, I stared at his desk. I realized I could read the referral slip upside down. The yard duty teacher had written: *Benched for one week.*

Theresa leaned toward me and whispered, remorsefully, "I guess we should be benched for two weeks." She felt worse than I had suspected.

I glared at her and shook my head no.

The principal put down the phone. "Well, young ladies?"

"We should be benched for a week," I blurted.

"I agree . . . and I don't want to see you back here anytime soon." He signed the referral and sent us back to class.

"How did you know to say one week?" Theresa asked on our way back to class.

"I could read what the yard duty teacher put on the slip. Upside down," I told her.

"Wow, you can read upside down?" Theresa said, her ponytail swinging like a pendulum.

I didn't answer her.

That night I told my mother that I fell, trying to jump rope double Dutch.

*　*　*

Theresa and I were confined at every recess and lunchtime to the same green bench next to the stucco wall of the cafeteria building. It was indisputably the Bad Kids' Bench. Kindergartners and first graders had to file by to get to their classrooms and they always gave us a wide berth, their orderly line snaking away from us, then back in formation, as if our badness might be contagious. The bench faced the playground so the entire recess population could see who was *not privileged* enough to play. The yard duty teacher could keep an eye on us, too, in case we decided to jump up and sneak in a hopscotch game. Indignant and humiliated, I refused to talk to Theresa, who didn't seem to have any inhibitions about being chatty.

She bragged to me about all sorts of things, but I was aloof until she said, "My mom takes me to the *big* downtown library every Tuesday after school."

I rode my bike to the small branch library near my house every weekend, but my parents both worked full-time and couldn't always manage after-school activities or driving to the main branch. The *big* library had a hundred times the selection of the branch library and a huge children's room with comfy pillows. They sometimes had puppet shows, story times, free bookmarks, and writing contests.

"Yep, every single Tuesday I go to the *big* downtown library to check out as many books as I like."

Before I could pretend I didn't care, I said, "You're lucky." I was suddenly jealous of Theresa, but I didn't want her to know how much. So I returned to my determined martyrdom. Instead of listening to her, I stared at the dirt and ignored her prattle.

The week was over soon enough. The principal never called my parents. The other kids didn't seem to care that I had been disciplined on the Bad Kids' Bench. In fact, I actually detected a subtle reverence from some of my classmates. From then on, Theresa left me alone and Mary Lou was my widely acknowledged ally. I didn't know how I'd ever repay her.

* * *

A few weeks passed and one of the girls in our class had a slumber party. All the fifth-grade girls were invited. The barrage of females descended on the birthday girl's house with sleeping bags, pillows, and overnight cases.

Mary Lou and I set up our sleeping bags right next to each other. The night progressed happily . . . until someone suggested we tell ghost stories.

I hated ghost stories. I had far too active of an imagination, which always took me much farther than the storytelling. I couldn't seem to turn off the dark, scary world. If I saw even a slightly scary movie on television, my stomach would churn for days and I'd have to sleep with my bedside lamp on all night. Mary Lou must have felt the same, because she moved closer to me. We huddled together behind the avid listeners with our pillows almost covering our faces. There was no way *not* to listen. One girl told a particularly gruesome tale about a tree whose giant branches turned into fingers and could grab and capture children. Most of the girls squealed and clutched one another in mock terror before they ended up giggling. Already fraught with anxiety, I couldn't imagine how I would get through the night. I suddenly wanted to be in my own house, in my own bed, with my parents down the hall and my trusty bedside lamp. There didn't seem to be any way out of the situation that wasn't humiliating. At least Mary Lou was by my side.

Suddenly, Mary Lou started crying. "I'm scared," she said. "I want to go home."

Mary Lou had read my mind but had voiced it with her own tears.

One of the girls said, "Don't be such a baby!"

Others chimed in, "Mary Lou's a scaredy-cat!"

"I'm calling my parents," said Mary Lou through her giant sniffles.

"The baby's calling her mommy and daddy," the girls chanted.

I shivered in my sleeping bag, my stomach sick with fear. Sick that Mary Lou was leaving. Sick that I was next to a window, with a tree looming on the other side.

Mary Lou headed toward the phone and didn't seem to care about the taunting. She called her parents with her chin up, set down the phone, and methodically began packing up her things.

My sleeping area looked bare without Mary Lou's sleeping bag and blanket. A tree branch brushed against the window from the wind. I was convinced it was the same tree from the story and that I would be its next victim.

I stood up and began rolling up my sleeping bag. "I'm going home, too. Mary Lou, can your dad give me a ride?"

I heard more giggles.

Then, from across the room, a small voice said, "Me, too?"

Mary Lou nodded.

I secretly celebrated. I knew that we'd suffer the consequences of the gossip and finger-pointing at school on Monday, but now I didn't care. There was safety in numbers. As I dragged my things into the hallway, I saw the third person.

It was Theresa.

The three of us huddled on the front porch waiting for Mary Lou's dad. In a final gesture of belittlement, one of the girls turned off the porch light so we had to wait on the front steps in the dark, directly under the tree with the sprawling branches. On the other side of the door, the party howled with laughter. I was never so grateful to see station wagon headlights.

Mary Lou's dad headed toward Theresa's house first. On the way, we were mostly quiet, but I felt happy. Happy I was going home to my own room. Happy that Mary Lou's tearful exit scene had been watered down by our group departure. I was puzzled, though, that Theresa had been frightened, too. She always seemed so confident, so tough.

In front of Theresa's house, she climbed out of the car and said, "So do you guys want to go to the *big* library with me after school on Tuesdays? My mom drives me and she could drive you, too."

I would love *to go to the* big *downtown library on Tuesdays after school*, I thought. *But with Theresa?* My mind battled with my emotions.

Theresa eagerly continued. "My mom can call your moms to . . . you know . . . make sure it's okay and everything."

I hesitated. "Are *you* going?" I asked Mary Lou.

"I can't," she said. "But you should go if you want to."

Theresa sounded sincere enough.

Mary Lou nudged me in the backseat as if to say, *Go!*

I finally nodded.

* * *

It was a strange camaraderie, given our history. Theresa and I shared many trips to the library together on Tuesdays. I've often wondered if, in some convoluted way, Theresa's abuse had been an attempt to get my attention. She liked the library and I always had my nose in a book, so she targeted me. Too bad for my legs that she didn't have better social skills!

Mary Lou is still my hero. If a person believes in the domino effect, the premise that one action triggers another, then I am deeply indebted to her. If she had never made me stand up to Theresa, I would have existed on the outskirts of fifth-grade society, always defenseless. I would have never gained Mary Lou's respect or become her friend. I wouldn't have gone home with her that night at the slumber party. Instead, I would have suffered through my worst imaginings. And if it weren't for Mary Lou, I might not have had the opportunity or courage to accept Theresa's invitation to the *big* library on Tuesdays, which fueled my affection for books in a dramatic way. After all, I was entering the enemy's camp.

It's sometimes easier to be brave if you have someone with whom you can stand beside or who you know is always standing behind you. Being Mary Lou's friend was always comforting, even when she revealed her own vulnerability. Big, strong people have fears (as do tiny, wiry people), and it often takes more courage to reveal a weakness than to cover it up. She was confident, determined, fair-minded, and unafraid of her emotions. I was her antithesis: naive, insecure, and desperately wanting to be a part of something. Mary Lou fit in because she didn't try to be anything but herself.

I wanted to be just like her.

MY BEST FRIEND
by Jennifer L. Holm

IT'S THE KIND OF DAY that if you leave an egg out it will fry in a second. By the time we reach the minimart my shirt is sticking to my back, my baby-sitting money is jangling in my pockets, and all I can think of is how good the chocolate is going to taste on my tongue.

"What do you want?" I ask.

Alexandra scrunches her mouth like she always does when she's trying to decide what flavor to get, but I know what she'll say before she says it.

"Creamsicle."

I go inside and fish out two ice-cream bars from the freezer, letting the cool air rush over me for a second. The same bald guy who is always there takes my money and I walk out, the door ringing behind me.

"Here you go," I say, passing her the ice-cream bar.

"Thanks," she says.

"Ready?" I say, and she nods, her red pigtails flopping. We suck hard.

"Oh," Alexandra groans. "I think my brain is frozen."

"Mine, too," I say, and we both laugh.

"What should we do today?" I ask.

"Let's look for alligators," Alexandra says. This is what she always says.

"There aren't any alligators here," I say.

I hear the door jangle open. The bald man is standing there with a strange look on his face.

"Who you talking to, kid?" he asks.

*   *   *

We moved here to Alligator Grove at the beginning of the summer and now it's almost August. We live in a shabby trailer that my mom said was a good deal because it came with a free bed. It's the third place we've lived this year, my mom and me, and it's the farthest south, in a part of Florida that no one's ever heard of, not like Orlando or Key West. My mom's friend Linda Sue had told her about the country club where she worked as a waitress.

"Linda Sue says I can make a hundred dollars in tips at lunch alone!" my mom had said as we drove in our old beat-up Toyota across the dusty roads of Arkansas.

I didn't say anything; I knew better. My mom is like this. She gets excited and the next thing I know my pink suitcase is in the back of the car and we are on the road, the miles stretching out before us like ribbon candy.

Our trailer is old, with blue-green siding that has faded to the color of the slime on the pool that no one uses. There's no other kids here except for Linda Sue's baby, Lulu, who is two and bites everything in sight, including me. She's worse than any dog I know.

My mom's sitting on the steps of the trailer smoking a cigarette when I come home. She's still got her uniform on from work: black polyester pants and a button-down white oxford shirt. Clip-on tie. Her beautiful red hair is pinned back in a bun, and it's sort of sagging in the humidity.

"Hi, honey," she says.

"How was work?" I ask.

My mom sighs. "Could be better. Thirty bucks in tips. I think things are slow because it's summer. Linda Sue says this is more of a resort area. You know, people come down in the winter and all."

I don't say anything.

"What'd you do today?"

I shrug. "I don't know. Stuff."

"Linda Sue asked if I wanted to go out for a drink with her tonight. Will you watch Lulu?"

"Do you have to?" I ask.

"No," she says. "But I'd like to." I can hear the hope in her voice.

I look down at my feet. "You can go. I'll watch Lulu."

She ruffles my hair. "Thanks, sweetie."

The sun is setting, turning the sky pink.

"Come on," she says with a smile, grinding out her cigarette. "Let's have dinner. I brought home hamburgers from the restaurant. Your favorite."

"Okay," I say, and follow her inside.

* * *

Shady Grove Trailer Park isn't the worst place we've lived, but it isn't the best, either. Most everyone here is old — retirees, my mom says, from places like Michigan and Illinois.

"Full of Midwesterners," she says, not approvingly. My dad was from Chicago, and since he ran out on us five years ago when I was six, Mom hasn't had much good to say about anyone from Chicago.

It's late afternoon and I walk over to the pool. It's all slimy green and you can't see the water.

Alexandra's already there, sitting on one of the old plastic chairs they leave out. She's wearing a lemon-yellow sundress and sandals, new ones, not like mine, which are from the leftover bin at a five-and-dime store and already falling apart.

"Hey," she says.

"Hey," I say back.

She holds out a brush. "Let's braid our hair."

"French braids?" I ask.

"Perfect," she says, and leans her head back.

Alexandra has thick red hair, beautiful, the kind of hair a princess in a movie has, or maybe Rapunzel.

"So what time did she get home?" Alexandra asks.

"Pretty late."

"Did they go to that bar out by the highway?"

I nod. "The Crazy Cowboy. I wish she wouldn't go out with Linda Sue."

"Yeah, she's kind of wild, isn't she?" Alexandra says.

"And there's always some guy around," I say.

This is why Alexandra is my best friend. I can tell her anything.

"Hi there," a voice says.

I look up, startled.

An old woman with pink-tinted hair is standing there, leaning on a walker. She's wearing a pink house-dress and holding an empty bread bag, like the kind Wonder Bread comes in.

"What have you got there?" the woman asks.

I feel the heavy weight of the brush in my hand.

"Nothing," I say quickly.

I hear my mom calling my name. "Leggy!"

The old woman looks at me, but I won't meet her eyes.

"I have to go," I say, and get up and walk quickly away.

When I look back, the old woman is still watching me.

*　*　*

"You sure you'll be okay today?" my mom asks.

I'm sitting on her bed watching her get dressed for work. She's pinning her hair up, her fingers nimble, like magic. Next, earrings, the pretty silvery dangly ones my dad gave her. They're the only things she kept.

"Sure," I say.

"I feel bad leaving you here all alone," she says.

"I don't mind," I tell her.

She turns to me, smooths the hair off my forehead. "Things'll be better when school starts, you know. You'll be able to make friends."

"I know," I say, because it's true. I will make friends, but I'll leave them in a few months when she gets it into her head to move again after someone calls promising the moon or a good job somewhere far away.

A slash of red lipstick and she is done. She blots her lips with a tissue.

"We're going to stick it out here; I promise," my mom says.

And because she is my mom and I love her, I say, "I know."

*　*　*

I sit at the edge of the pool. Alexandra sits next to me.

"Want to go to the minimart and get ice-cream bars?" she asks.

"It's too hot to walk that far," I say. And then I can't help it. "I hate this place."

"It's not so bad," she says. "It's better than that town in Arkansas. Remember how weird the house smelled?"

I giggle. "Like toe jam."

She giggles back. "Or dirty underwear." Alexandra wiggles her toes in her sandals. "Let's dip our feet in the water."

"Okay," I say, and begin to unbuckle the straps of my sandals.

"I wouldn't do that if I were you," a voice says.

I turn around to see the pink-haired lady standing there, leaning on her walker, the bread bag in her hand.

"Why not?" I ask.

She digs her hand into the bag and pulls out a hunk of what looks like raw hamburger. She tosses it into the air and it lands in the pool with a plop.

Suddenly there is a huge splash and I scramble to my feet.

"An alligator!" I gasp, watching as the big mouth opens and closes over the floating hamburger.

The old lady chuckles. "That's just Big Al. He's lived there forever."

"Does he eat people?"

"Not lately," she says, settling herself in a plastic chair.

"Wow," I say, watching as the eyes slide beneath the surface, disappearing in the slimy water. "No wonder no one ever uses this pool."

The old woman looks at me. "You new here?"

"The blue-green trailer."

She nods knowingly. "Next to the kid who bites. What's your name?"

"Allegra," I say. "But everyone calls me Leggy."

"Dorenda," she says. "My mother named me after her best friends, Doris and Brenda."

"Dorenda," I say. "That's a neat name."

She reaches into the pocket of her pink housecoat and pulls out a handful of saltwater taffy. "Want one? The peppermint ones are good."

I take one and unwrap it. It's sticky but melts on my tongue.

"My doctor says I'm not supposed to eat sweets, but

I'm not too good at following the rules," she says and squints up to the sun. "So, Leggy, how are you liking Alligator Grove?"

"It's okay, I guess."

"Kind of quiet, huh? I'm from New York City, and believe you me, this sure is quiet after that town."

"It is pretty quiet," I agree. "But Alexandra says it isn't as bad as some places."

"Alexandra," Dorenda says, trying it out on her tongue. "Now that's a pretty name."

"Her full name is Alexandra Sorge."

"What's she like, this Alexandra Sorge?"

The words leave my mouth before I can stop them. "She's my best friend. She's got red hair and is real nice. We do everything together."

"I had red hair when I was your age, but now I get mine from Miss Clairol," Dorenda says with a chuckle.

"Alexandra's is real," I say. "Sometimes I braid it for her. French braids."

"She sounds like my friend Lara Ann. I had a friend named Lara Ann when I was your age. Boy, did we ever used to get into trouble."

The feeling wells up inside of my chest and I blurt out, "Alexandra's not a real person. I made her up. She's an imaginary friend."

Dorenda looks at me and I wait for her to tell me that I'm crazy or worse.

Instead she says, "So what? I talk to Big Al all the time. He's a real good listener."

I let this sink in.

"He ever try to bite you?" I ask.

"Nah. He's an old guy. Sometimes he'll sunbathe on the concrete."

"Huh," I say.

"A person's just got to talk sometimes. And believe you me, I'm a woman with opinions. You got opinions?"

"I guess," I say.

"That's good." Dorenda stands up, grasps her walker. "Now, I've got some lemonade cooling in the fridge. Why don't you go fetch it here and we can sit around and share our opinions? How does that sound?"

I hesitate and then say, "Okay."

Like she says, a person's just got to talk sometimes.

CONNIE HUNTER WILLIAMS, PSYCHIC TEACHER
by Meg Cabot

CONNIE HUNTER WAS THE BEST TEACHER I EVER HAD. All of my friends — the ones who got stuck with the OTHER fourth-grade teachers (who had wobbly necks, orthopedic shoes, husbands, and wore their hair in buns) at Elm Heights Elementary School — were jealous of me. Because Mrs. Hunter had feathered AND frosted hair, wore go-go boots with miniskirts, and was DIVORCED. Not to mention that nothing about her was at all wobbly.

I knew Mrs. Hunter was going to turn out to be my favorite teacher of all time when, for the last ten minutes of the first day of class, she took out a copy of *The Boxcar Children* (which happened to be my favorite series at the time) and began to read aloud to us. Every day, from three o'clock until the bell rang at three ten, Mrs. Hunter would read to us. Sometimes, if the weather was horrible and we had to stay indoors, she'd read to us during recess as well.

Occasionally, between books, Mrs. Hunter would

tell us stories. The stories were mostly about predictions she'd made that either had come true already or were about to.

It turned out that Mrs. Hunter, before she'd started teaching fourth and fifth grades, had been an actual, practicing psychic. Among some of the successful predictions she made during the school year were:

a) various jet crashes
b) the energy crisis
c) the blizzard of '78
d) the Hoosiers' winning season
e) that Judy Grubb would break her arm on the teeter-totter if she wasn't more careful

I had several personal brushes with Mrs. Hunter's psychic abilities. The first time was midway through my fourth-grade year, when a new girl joined our class. Her name was as exotic as the place from which she'd moved — Shoshona. And she was from Canada.

Being Canadian, Shoshona had some fancy ways compared to us Hoosiers. It was Shoshona who introduced our class to the titillating concept of "going together." She and Jeff Niehardt were "going together" by the end of Shoshona's first day at Elm Heights. It didn't take much longer than that for the rest of the class to pair up.

Everyone except for me. I didn't want to "go with" anyone.

This horrified Shoshona. She suggested I "go with" Joey Meadows, a fifth grader who liked *The Boxcar Children* as much as I did (something he would only admit when there were no other males within hearing distance).

Nice as I found Joey, I wasn't ready for that kind of commitment. I just wanted to dig holes in the dirt, my hobby at the time.

So I gently turned down Joey's kind (read: pity) offer to "go with" me and went back to digging my holes.

Little did I know how this simple act would enrage Shoshona. The very next day when I came to school, I was no longer Meggin Cabot. According to Shoshona, I was now Maggot Cabbage and would remain so until I changed my mind and decided to "go with" Joey Meadows.

I didn't cry in front of her. I had more pride than that. But I spent plenty of hours in my bedroom closet, weeping as if my heart would break. I didn't want to be called Maggot Cabbage for the rest of my life. But then, I didn't want to "go with" anybody, either.

The very next day, at three o'clock, instead of reading a chapter from *The Boxcar Children* or telling us about the time she spared a young couple from certain death by instructing them not to go to Guatemala on their honeymoon, Mrs. Hunter looked at us sternly and told us that she understood that there were children in her class who were "going together."

Never, Mrs. Hunter said, had she heard of anything more ridiculous. Fourth graders, she said, do not "go together." She added that if she heard any more reports of children "going together" she would send the offenders to Mrs. Harrigan, the principal — a fate, needless to say, worse than death.

Alarmed — thinking Shoshona would assume I tattled and I'd be Maggot Cabbage forevermore — I watched as Jeff Niehardt sadly erased Shoshona's name from the inside of his pencil box. Shoshona swore at recess that when she and Jeff turned eighteen, no one, not even Mrs. Harrigan, would stop them from going together.

It turned out I needn't have worried. No one questioned how Mrs. Hunter found out. She was psychic, after all.

And no one called me Maggot Cabbage ever again.

Fourth grade ended on such a high note — Shoshona even moved back to Canada — that I never expected fifth grade could possibly exceed it. But it did. Because, miracle of miracles, I got Mrs. Hunter as a teacher AGAIN.

On the first day of school, she called me in from recess and asked me gravely if I would do her the great favor of sitting in the last row between Mike Boisson and Stuart Bogue, who were the class's biggest troublemakers. She hoped my "positive energy" would rub off on them.

Was it Mrs. Hunter's psychic powers that told her Stuart Bogue was the one boy in the entire school who, if he'd asked me the year before, I would have agreed to "go with"? Because Stuart was the only boy at Elm Heights who liked digging holes as much as I did. (In his case, he was looking for snakes, not the tiny elusive dirt people I was convinced lived down there. But I was willing to let this pass.)

Oh, what a blissful year fifth grade turned out to be! Sitting all day long next to Stuart Bogue — sending him and Mike Boisson scathing looks when they swapped booger jokes during math — then helping Stuart dig for snakes (and dirt people) at recess . . . could a girl ask for anything more?

But it got better. On the day Mrs. Hunter took the fifth-grade class to Western Skateland, Stuart actually asked me to skate with him during Couples Only

Snowball Skate. I smiled so much and so hard that day — I couldn't help it; I was THAT happy — I thought my lips would crack in two.

Romance was in the air. Because that was the year a huge bouquet arrived for Mrs. Hunter during math and she curiously removed the card (I guess this was one time her psychic warning system faltered), then showed it to me with fingers trembling for joy, since I happened to be the person nearest her. *Will you marry me?* the card said.

I guess Mrs. Hunter's answer was yes, because when we came back from winter break, her name was Mrs. Williams.

Only a single dark cloud marred my second year with Mrs. Williams. And that was the curious habit she had of forcing me to rewrite every story I turned in to her. Mrs. Williams enjoyed assigning creative writing projects almost as much as I loved doing them. But, oddly, while she would pass back everyone else's stories with a check or check plus on them, she would always write *See Me* on mine.

Then, just before recess, when I'd go to her desk to *See Her*, Mrs. Williams would point out places where the story might be strengthened or scenes I might want to think about leaving out. Then she'd ask me to rewrite it. Sometimes seven or eight times. The *same story*.

No one else in the class ever had to rewrite their stories. When my other classmates asked me why I was doing it, I'd shrug and say, "Because Mrs. Williams told me to." It wasn't until the end of the school year, when we were all going off to Binford Middle School — all except for Stuart, who was moving to Milwaukee, taking my heart with him, never to return it (well, until ninth grade, anyway) — that it finally occurred to me to ask Mrs. Williams why she'd made me rewrite all of my stories so many times.

"I know how you hate it, Meg," she explained. "But it's something you're going to be doing a lot in your future. So you need to get used to it."

Back then, I'd assumed she'd meant that rewriting was something they made you do a lot in sixth grade.

Only they didn't. Not in middle school, and not in high school — or even college.

It wasn't until recently that I realized what Mrs. Williams must have known: that someday, I would become a writer and rewriting my stories — sometimes what seemed like endlessly — would be the part of the job that I'd hate most.

But she was right: Because of her, I was used to it.

And if I knew where she was today, I'd thank her for it.

SQUIRREL
by Ann M. Martin

I AM AN OLD DOG NOW. My fur has begun to turn white, even in the places where it was once blackest black. One eye is filmy, the hearing is gone from my right ear, and my joints creak and crack. Sometimes I can't make the jump from the floor onto Susan's bed, and then Susan has to bend over and lift me up, her own joints creaking. "Just look at us," she says. "An old woman and an old dog. Two ancient ladies, deaf and gray." She lowers me onto the bed, then sits down next to me with a sigh and reaches out to rub my belly. I recall those days long ago when Mother taught me to fear humans. I roll over and give Susan's hand a lick.

"Two ancient ladies," Susan says again.

*   *   *

So this is what it's like to be old. Deaf and gray and slow and creaky. At least this is what it's like for me. I can't speak for all dogs, of course, since not all dogs are alike. And, most certainly, not all dogs have the same experiences. I've known dogs who dined on fine foods and led pampered lives, sleeping on soft beds and being served hamburger and chicken and even steak. I've known dogs who looked longingly at warm homes, who were not invited inside, who stayed in a garage or a shed or a drainage ditch for a few days, then moved on. I've known dogs who were treated cruelly by human hands and dogs who were treated with the gentlest touch, dogs who starved and dogs who grew fat from too many treats. I've known all these dogs, and I've been all these dogs.

*   *   *

We were born in a wheelbarrow, my brother and I. Our mother was looking for a place that was warm, dry, safe from coyotes and other predators, and hidden from humans. The wheelbarrow, filled with straw, was all of these things. Mother (her dog name was Stream, but to Bone and me she was simply Mother) gave birth to us in late winter, just as the days were starting to turn warm. It was a time when the people who owned the big house in the country might need a wheelbarrow. But they wouldn't need *this* wheelbarrow, which was old and rusty and had been hastily stowed in a corner of a little-used shed the previous winter.

Mother gave birth to five puppies, but only Bone

and I survived. Two of the puppies were born dead, and a third lived for less than an hour. When, after our first night, Mother saw that Bone and I were still strong and active and nursing well, she gave us our names. She chose, as mother dogs do, names of things that were important to her. So I was known as Squirrel and my brother was known as Bone.

What I remember of those first days in the wheelbarrow is comfort. Bone and I were warm, very warm, and we lay nestled against Mother, listening to her heartbeat. When Mother left the wheelbarrow for food, we nestled against each other or burrowed in the straw. I could hear Bone's heartbeat, too.

As Bone and I grew, we became aware of the bigger world of the shed, and soon our wheelbarrow began to feel like an island. Our heads and legs stopped wobbling and our eyes were able to focus, and now we could peer over the edge of the wheelbarrow. We saw the cats who shared the shed with us. There were mice, too, lots of them. The mice ate corn and seeds, the cats ate the mice, and sometimes owls or hawks caught and ate the cats. For the time being, Bone and I didn't have to worry about any of that. Mother fed us. Mother protected us. Bone and I watched the shed world from our island; we never left the wheelbarrow.

*　*　*

But Mother left the wheelbarrow at regular times each day — to find food and to relieve herself. The people who owned the big house didn't know that a dog was living on their property. And Mother sensed that they wouldn't *want* to know that a dog was living on their property. She hunted for food in secret, keeping herself well hidden from the house.

One day, when the air blew warm through the windows of the shed and brought sweet fragrances to Bone and me, making our noses twitch, Mother nudged us over the edge of the wheelbarrow. She nudged Bone first, because he was a boy, and then me. Bone landed on a stack of burlap sacks, and I landed on top of him. I looked back up at Mother, at our little island, and I let out a whimper. But not Bone. Bone scampered to the floor. Then, tail held high, he began to investigate the shed. I followed him. Mother followed us.

Mother allowed Bone and me to investigate all we wanted, as long as we stayed in the shed — or behind the shed, out of view of the house. Behind the shed was much more interesting than in the shed. Behind the shed was Outdoors. The more we investigated, the braver I felt, but only when Bone was in front of me. With Bone in front, his tail high, my own tail was held high. With Bone out of sight, I was lost.

The more time Bone and I spent out of the shed, the less we nursed. Mother brought us scraps of food and showed us how to hunt. One morning Mother disappeared, leaving Bone and me playing beside a stone wall. When she returned, she was carrying something wonderful-smelling, but she wouldn't share it with us. With the something still in her mouth, she turned and walked away, looking at us over her shoulder from time to time, keeping close to a row of bushes.

Bone knew what Mother wanted, and he followed her. I followed Bone, as usual. The farther I walked, the more my nose twitched. I could smell whatever Mother was carrying, and lots more.

Mother led us to garbage, to a lovely pile of old chicken and stale bread and bits of scrambled egg and three olives and congealed spaghetti and a puddle of sour milk.

Bone and I pounced. Mother had shown us how a dog could hunt even when there were no animals to hunt for. This was heaven.

That night, our stomachs full of scraps, Bone and I lay curled up in the shed with Mother, listening to the wind, listening to her heartbeat. The next morning, Mother trotted out of the shed, in the direction of the garbage.

She never came back.

*　*　*

Bone and I were on our own. We were responsible for finding all of our food and water and for remembering the many, many things Mother had taught us — how to stay out of trouble, when to snap and bite at an animal, to steer clear of humans and other dogs, to clean our wounds, to groom ourselves. We tried our best and we managed fairly well. The garbage heap became our best friend. But Bone and I had noticed something: The warmer the weather became, the more we saw the people who lived in the house. They worked outside and ate outside, and the children played outside. It became harder and harder to sneak to the garbage pile. Bone started visiting it at night, but that was worse. The owls were out then, and I could hear coyotes yipping in the hills.

It was on a summer day, at a time when the afternoons were hot, but the nights were beginning to feel chilly, that Bone decided to leave. He woke up early one morning when the nighttime creatures were going to sleep, but before the humans had awakened. He rolled off of our burlap bed, touched my nose with his, then slipped through the open door of the shed and out into the quiet. I stood in the doorway watching him and saw that he looked at me over his shoulder from time to time. He trotted along the row of bushes and paused at the garbage pile. When he kept on going, I ran after him.

Bone heard me coming and waited for me to catch up, as he always did, and then we trotted along shoulder to shoulder until I realized we were as far from the big house as we had ever been. We walked through woods and a field and more woods and then we came to a road with lots and lots of cars flying along it. Bone and I had seen cars drive up to the big house before, but just one or two at a time. Those cars moved very slowly. But these cars, each of them, went by with a roar and a whoosh of wind.

Bone looked ready to bolt across the road and hope for the best when suddenly a car pulled to the side of the road and screeched to a stop. While other drivers honked their horns, two people, a woman and a man, jumped out of the car and ran to Bone and me. Before we knew it, they had scooped us into their arms.

"Oh, look. They're just puppies!" the woman cried. "I wonder what they're doing way out here."

"I don't know," said the man. "But come on back to the car before we get ourselves killed."

*　*　*

This was how Bone and I found our first home with humans. We didn't last long there. We had never lived with people, of course, and we hadn't lived indoors. We were used to relieving ourselves whenever and wherever we pleased. On our very first night in the house I made a puddle on a rug and the woman smacked me on my nose. When Bone made a puddle and she smacked him, he bared his teeth and bit her.

The man watched this with his arms crossed and said, "They're feral, Marcy. This isn't going to work."

The next morning there were more puddles and messes, especially after Bone tipped over the kitchen garbage pail to get our breakfast.

"Out!" shouted the woman when she found us in the potato peelings and bits of hamburger and opened tea bags and crumbs from a coffee cake. "*Bad* dogs!"

That afternoon, when the woman wasn't at home, the man tossed Bone and me into the car, started the engine with a roar, and drove away very fast. He drove until he came to a place with a line of buildings, lots of cars standing still in rows, and lots of people carrying paper bags.

Sweating, the man rolled down his window, grabbed

first Bone, then me, threw us out, and drove away, all without bothering to stop the car.

Bone landed hard, his snout smashing against the pavement, and he couldn't help letting out a cry of pain. I landed several feet away from him, on my shoulder. I heard a small crack, but I was too stunned to yelp. I didn't even move. After a moment, I tried to stand, but my leg gave way and I sank down again. I looked at Bone. He was limping toward me, his nose bloody, and he had almost reached me when I heard someone cry, "Did you see that? Someone threw those puppies out of a car!"

"Are they all right?" asked someone else.

Two women, their arms loaded with heavy bags, ran to us. They dropped the bags and knelt down.

"I think they're going to be okay," said one.

"Look how cute this one is," said the other, motioning to Bone. "The tan one. I always wanted a puppy. I'm going to take it home."

"What about the spotted one?"

"Well, I don't think I can manage two dogs. And that one isn't as cute. I'll just take this one."

"And leave the other one here?"

"It'll be all right. Someone else will come along and find it. That's why they were dumped at the mall, you know."

The women gathered up their bags and walked off with Bone, wiping his nose with a Kleenex as they went.

And that is how I was separated from my brother.

*   *   *

Bone was gone. I didn't know what to do. For a few minutes I sat on the pavement in the spot where I had landed. After a while I realized that the pain in my shoulder wasn't as bad as before. I tried standing up and found that although it hurt a bit, I could walk. I made my way to the shade of a tree and sat down. I was thirsty, so I looked around for a brook or a stream. I didn't see one, but I found a puddle at the edge of the pavement and had a drink from that. Then I sat down again.

Mother had taught Bone and me to be wary of people. I was also wary of cars now, and with so many of them around I was afraid to move. I made myself very still and small under the tree. All afternoon I watched people and cars come and go. No one noticed me. The light began to fade, and soon I realized that more cars were leaving than arriving. By the time darkness fell, only a handful of cars were left. And I was very hungry.

With a sigh, wondering where Bone was, wondering where Mother was, I took another drink from the puddle. Mother was truly gone; I felt sure of that. Something had happened and she had died. That was the only reason she would leave Bone and me when we were so young. But Bone . . . Bone could be somewhere nearby. Maybe he had a home with the woman with all the bags; maybe he didn't. After all, his first home with people hadn't worked out. Maybe Bone was looking for me right now. Maybe he was trying to make his way back to this place where we had been thrown away.

But I couldn't stay here. The water in the puddle wouldn't last, and I needed food. I glanced around, sniffed the air, then left my tree. Garbage was my best chance for a meal, and I found lots of it behind the row of buildings the people had been going in and out of. A trash can had been tipped over and I was rooting through the garbage, having just caught the scent of chicken, when I heard a low growl behind me. Without even turning to see what was growling, I ran.

I ran and ran, avoiding cars, and didn't stop until I had come to a quieter place, a small area that was wooded, but still in sight of people and cars and buildings. I fell asleep in the woods that night, my stomach empty, my mouth dry, wishing for our old bed in the wheelbarrow, wishing for Bone, wishing to hear Mother's heartbeat.

* * *

Those woods became my home. I stayed there for a long time, for as long as it takes for the leaves on the trees to change color, to drop off; for the snows to fall, then melt; for the leaves to emerge again; and for my legs to grow long. I found garbage and other things to eat, although never enough; I was always just a little hungry. I hid when I saw dogs; I hid when I saw people.

I was very lonely.

One evening when the air was warm again and the trees were heavy with new leaves, I ventured to the edge of my woods. I hadn't eaten much in several days and I needed to find a good garbage heap, one that was big and well stocked but not difficult to get to. One side of the woods bordered a highway. The highway was busy, but if I could cross it, I would reach a row of garbage cans that were often left partially open.

I stood by the side of the highway, watching headlights stream by and thinking that even though my stomach was growling, maybe I should wait just a few more hours until the quiet of full night. I was watching the headlights when I noticed another dog standing at the edge of the road watching headlights, concentrating on the traffic. I was about to turn and run when I saw that the dog was tan like Bone, had Bone's face, was

Bone grown up, with legs as long as mine, proud tail —
now fat and fluffy — held high in the air.

I crept toward him, then let out a yip of joy.

At my yip, the other dog turned quickly but didn't
bark, just watched my approach. And I could tell, from
several feet away, that this wasn't Bone after all. This dog
was female. I jumped back and let out a growl, but the
dog wagged her tail at me and put her rump in the air,
and her chest and front legs on the ground. Then she
dropped her rump and crawled toward me on her belly.

I approached her again slowly, sniffed at her snout,
and my own tail began to wag.

My new friend was named Moon, and she did look
very much like Bone, or at least the way Bone might
look now that he was grown. And she was as brave as
Bone had been. But I discovered something: In the time
I had been on my own, I had become braver. Maybe I
wasn't as brave as Bone and Moon, but I had done lots
of things on my own — scary things, things I did not
want to do — so I knew I was brave, too.

This is why, when Moon decided to move on, to
leave the little woods by the mall, I went with her.
Maybe Moon was older than I was or maybe she was
simply more adventurous, but she did not want to stay
put. She wanted to travel.

So we traveled. We traveled during the time the leaves turned colors again. We traveled during the snows. (We didn't travel quite as much during the snows, but we were on the move.) We were still traveling — now side by side, shoulder to shoulder — when the world became fresh and new again. And it was on one of these spring days with warm air and familiar country scents that we came to a sleepy lane and spotted a chipmunk perched on a fallen log on the other side. Moon sprinted across the road, and I was after her in a flash. Neither of us saw the truck that rounded the bend in the road; not until it was almost upon us. It hit Moon at high speed and sent her flying. She landed on the other side of the road in the woods and lay very still. The truck only clipped me, but it clipped the shoulder that had been injured when Bone and I were thrown away so long before, and I couldn't move, so I lay in the road. I was yelping for Moon, waiting for her to answer, when I realized that the truck that had hit us had come to a stop. I heard doors slamming, heard voices shouting, and soon arms were around me and a boy was saying, "This one's alive. I think it's going to be okay."

There was silence for a moment, and then another voice said, "This one's dead, I think, but let's take both of them to the vet."

And Moon and I were placed gently in the back of the truck. I fell asleep.

*   *   *

Moon was dead. The vet told the people who had hit us that she probably died instantly. My leg was broken, but it could be repaired. "I'll spay her for you, too," said the vet, "since she seems to be a stray. And I'll give her all her shots."

I stayed at the vet's for what seemed a very long time — as long as it took for the moon to change from a sliver to a half circle. Then the people who had brought me to the vet came back and put me in their truck. As we drove away, a boy said, "You're going to be our dog for the summer. Your name will be Daisy. Remember the dog we had last summer, Mom? Sasha was a good dog."

"Sasha wasn't our last-summer dog," said a girl. "Last summer's was Shadow. Sasha was two summers ago."

"Oh, yeah," said the boy.

The people fixed me up in their garage with a bed and a dish of food and a bowl of water. And, just like at the vet's, I didn't have to worry about finding garbage. Every morning and every evening someone from the house came out to the garage and filled the dish with table scraps. And the girl and the boy patted me and played with me and showed me where I could relieve myself.

When my leg had healed completely I began to explore the yard around the people's house. At first I was reluctant to leave the garage, which reminded me of the old shed in the country. But soon the scents and sounds of the summertime called to me, and I ventured outside to the grass and gardens and bees and bugs. Sometimes I peeked through the front door of the house, eager for company, and someone would call out, "Hi, Daisy!" but the door was never opened for me.

The weather grew cooler, and I discovered something disappointing. I could no longer count on my food dish being filled twice a day. Sometimes it remained empty. A day or so would pass and then the woman in the family would run into the garage saying, "Oh, here, Daisy. We forgot all about you!" She would smile at me, but she did not often pat me. Hungry as I was, I always watched her disappear into the house before I turned to the table scraps.

One morning, not long after I had noticed the first change of color in the leaves, the people loaded a lot of boxes and suitcases into their truck and drove away.

When they had been gone for five days and five nights and my dishes had been empty for as long, I decided to leave.

This time there was no Bone to follow, no Moon to follow, and that was fine with me. I could take care of myself. And I did. For many, many changes of season — until the warm weather and the cold weather had come and gone so often that my black fur had turned white and my eyes were filmy and my joints creaked and I was an old dog.

* * *

I didn't usually nose around so close to the houses of humans, but I was tired, and I had found a nice quiet house far out in the country with a dish of water on the front porch. And I had watched the house long enough to know that an old woman lived there and that she put the water out just for me.

One morning when I crept up to the door I found a dish of food next to the water. It wasn't just any food. It was chicken cut up into small squares, mixed with rice and bits of cheese and some crunchy things I had eaten at the vet's.

The next morning there was more food. On the morning after that, while I was eating a bowl of steak and peas, the door opened a crack, and I saw the old woman. I stiffened, then backed up, and the woman said, "Oh, now. For heaven's sake, dog, you're as old as I am. Why don't you come inside and warm up?"

I was afraid to and I ran off, but the next morning the old woman appeared again and as she set out a dish of chicken and crunchies she said, "You know, the last thing I need is a dog, but I really think you ought to come inside." And she held the door open. "Come on, old dog," she said a moment later. "Enough of this silliness."

But I couldn't go into her house. Not until the morning when the air was so bitterly cold that I couldn't feel the bottoms of my paws. That morning, when the woman opened her door, I padded inside and lay down before a fire. The woman said to me, "We had better introduce ourselves, dog. My name is Susan. And I expect you have a name of your own already, but I don't know what it is, so I'm going to call you Addie. I hope that's okay with you."

Susan and I have lived together ever since. Every now and then I make a puddle on the floor instead of outdoors, but Susan doesn't seem to mind. She just says, "Outdoors, Addie, please." Every morning and every evening we eat together in her kitchen. At night, we sleep in Susan's bed. We ride in the car and take walks and recently Susan whispered to me, "Remember when

I said the last thing I needed was a dog? Well, that wasn't true. I do need you, and I'm glad you're here."

We're sitting side by side on the couch when she says this, and I slide into Susan's lap and heave a huge sigh. Many years ago, I thought my life would be whole if I could just find Bone again. But I didn't find him. And Mother was gone and Moon was gone, so finally I decided I was complete on my own. Then I found Susan. (When she tells the story, she says she found me.) I didn't think I needed a human any more than Susan thought she needed a dog. It turned out that there was room in my heart for a human after all.

The long-ago days of Mother and Bone and the shed have become fuzzy and have blended with images of Moon, of my travels, of other houses, of hiding places, of the vet — a tangle of memories leading to Susan. I press myself into her side and listen to her heartbeat. With my eyes closed, I might be in the straw-filled wheelbarrow again, nestled against Mother, listening to the first heartbeat I knew. I open my eyes and tilt my head back to look at Susan's lined face. She smiles, and scratches me behind the ears.

YOU COULDN'T HELP BUT NOTICE ELIZABETH LARUE. She was the one wearing black patent-leather shoes and a boy-band fan club jacket on the first day of school. And even though I was wearing the expression I'd practiced in the mirror all summer before coming to the Lane School — my too-cool-to-be-bothered look — she noticed me, too.

She made a beeline for me in homeroom and started asking questions like one of those guys on *60 Minutes*.

"Are you new?" she asked. "Me, too!"

I didn't have time to figure out how she knew I was new if she was, too; I scarcely had time to nod between questions.

"Do you take Spanish?" she asked. "Me, too!"

"Are you in Math A or B?" she asked. "I bet you're in A. Maybe we can be homework buddies."

"Do you like Justin Timberlake?" Without warning, she burst into the chorus of "Cry Me a River."

I pretended that I'd developed a sudden, intense

interest in picking off the nail polish I'd put on the night before. In the meantime, I peeked out from under my bangs to see if anyone was looking.

A knot of blond girls with their uniform skirts rolled up to the same identical height — 2.5 rows of plaid — were giggling and pointing at Elizabeth. I knew what they were saying about her. That she was a dork, that she was a loser, that she was a freak.

I knew because at my old school I was an Elizabeth LaRue. And I wasn't about to let that happen again. Especially not at the Lane School, this private all-girls school that my parents couldn't really afford but which they finally said I could go to after I begged them for a fresh start.

"You wanna walk to Spanish together?" she asked.

I shrugged.

"You wanna hang out at lunch?"

Elizabeth LaRue didn't look like other girls at the Lane School. She was pudgy and her bangs were cut straight across high on her forehead. Instead of looking cool or ironic or bored, she had a big, exaggerated smile that looked like it was painted on. She reminded me of a Lego woman. She wasn't the kind of person you sit with on the first day if you're trying to make a fresh start.

"I don't think so," I said.

"That's okay," she said brightly. "I'm sitting with Tabby, anyhow. Maybe tomorrow."

*   *   *

Tabby, it turned out, was Tabby Lane. She was this superskinny girl with perfectly straight white-blond hair and icy blue eyes. When she wasn't sitting across the lunch table from Elizabeth, Tabby Lane was at the center of the knot of blond girls with the identically short skirts. She was also one of *The* Lanes, the family that had started the Lane School. I couldn't understand why someone like Tabby Lane ate lunch with someone like Elizabeth, but I decided I needed to be friends with Tabby.

So after a week of trying (usually without success) to avoid Elizabeth in homeroom and Spanish and Math A and a week of eating by myself or skipping lunch and hiding out in a stall in the bathroom so I didn't have to eat by myself, I put my lunch tray down next to Elizabeth's.

"Oooh, goody," she said. "You decided to sit with us after all." She nudged Tabby, who was silently pushing her green beans around on her plate. "Tab, this is Margaret. She's new."

"Meg," I explained to Tabby. "They have me listed as Margaret, but I hate that name."

Tabby Lane peered out from behind a curtain of white-blond bangs that had fallen in a perfectly random, perfectly perfect way across her face. "Whatever."

"Tabby's my cousin," Elizabeth said. She beamed.

Tabby blew out a little puff of air with her lower lip; the hair that had fallen across her face floated in the air for a second, then settled back in place.

"C'mon," Elizabeth said to Tabby. "Eat a little bit more."

Tabby didn't even glance up.

"At least eat some of your salad. Or a carrot stick."

Tabby shot her a look. And I understood then why someone like Tabby Lane ate lunch with Elizabeth. Tabby had some kind of eating disorder. Elizabeth was there to make sure she ate.

As if she could read my mind, Tabby confirmed my theory. "Our parents make us eat together," she said flatly.

Elizabeth turned red. Then she looked down and tugged on a loose thread on the sleeve of her jacket.

Tabby sighed. "How much longer do we have, anyway?" she said, pulling back the sleeve of her uniform blouse. A delicate silver watch, something that looked more like a piece of jewelry than a watch, dangled from her pale, tiny wrist.

"I like your watch," I said.

"This?" She regarded the watch absentmindedly. "It's no big deal. It was, you know, in the family."

I didn't know, but I acted like I did.

She checked the time. "We still have ten minutes," she said. "Let's go have a smoke."

Smoking was forbidden at the Lane School. The penalty, according to the little plaid student handbook, was suspension.

Elizabeth's Lego smile disappeared. "Tab, you know we're not allowed."

Tabby blew on her bangs again. Then she looked at me. "You coming?"

I nodded. I'd never smoked before, but I wasn't going to let a little plaid rule book stand in the way of getting to be friends with Tabby Lane.

I got up and trailed after her, trying to copy the way she scuffed her clogs carelessly across the cafeteria floor. Elizabeth jumped up, too, and followed us, the heels of her patent-leather shoes tapping out what sounded to me like Morse code for SOS.

We followed Tabby out of the cafeteria, down a flight of steps, then down a dark hall next to the music room, until we were in a skinny passageway between the music room and the chapel. At the far end was a nook where choir robes were hanging on a row of pegs.

Tabby peered around the corner. Then she pulled a pack of Marlboros out of her purse. I slipped a cigarette out of the pack just the way she did, then held it between my fingers the way she did.

Elizabeth looked miserable, but she took a cigarette, too, then immediately dropped it on the floor. When she straightened up, her face was red. Her hand was shaking as she put the cigarette in her mouth.

Tabby fished around in her purse and brought out a red plastic lighter. She flicked it expertly and a yellow-blue flame shot up. Then she held the lighter out toward me. I understood, somehow, that this was part of the deal. I had to take the first drag. So I did.

The smoke tickled my throat — it was surprisingly hot — but I held back the urge to cough. I exhaled the way people do on TV.

It was Elizabeth's turn next. She puckered her lips and pulled her cheeks in so that she looked like a fish. Then she sucked on the cigarette. Instantly, her eyes bugged out and she started coughing and choking. Tears ran down her cheeks as she gasped for air.

Tabby looked vaguely amused. Then she lit her own

cigarette, drew in a long, deep breath, held it, and exhaled a perfect white stream of smoke.

I made a mental note of how she did this.

Elizabeth dropped her cigarette on the floor and stubbed it out under her shoe. "Sorry, Tab." She shrugged. "I just can't."

Tabby took another drag on her cigarette. I took another drag. Tabby exhaled. I exhaled.

Elizabeth waved her hand in front of her face, trying to fan the smoke away. Then she looked at her watch. "Hurry up," she said. "Big Beef could walk right through here any minute."

Tabby didn't blink.

I didn't know who Big Beef was, but I also didn't blink.

Elizabeth turned to me to explain. "Big Beef is Mrs. Neville," she said helpfully. "We call her that because she looks like a cow."

I almost burst out laughing. Mrs. Neville *did* look like a cow. But Tabby looked bored.

I decided to also look bored. "I know," I said.

* * *

I sat with Tabby and Elizabeth every day for the rest of that week. And every day when Tabby was done not eating, we went down to the cloakroom where Tabby and I smoked and Elizabeth kept watch for Big Beef.

"Have you ever noticed about Beef?" Elizabeth said. "She wears shoes like nurses do, the ones with squishy bottoms so she can sneak up on you."

"Liz," said Tabby, "you're such a moodle."

Elizabeth beamed, like this was a compliment. And, judging from the way Tabby had just called her Liz, not Elizabeth, maybe it was.

"Liz" tickled Tabby under her chin and said she was a moodle, too. Tabby tickled her back.

I stood there feeling invisible.

It was Elizabeth who finally noticed. "It's a family thing," she explained for my benefit. "It goes back to when we were little. We call each other moodles all the time."

* * *

After that, I decided I needed to do something alone with Tabby, not something that involved Elizabeth, too. That day, at the end of school, I saw Tabby in the hallway leaning against her locker with a couple of her friends with their identically short skirts.

"Hey, Tabby," I said.

She didn't look too excited to see me.

"Who's that?" said one of her friends, a girl who had long blond hair like Tabby's and who I knew, from gym class, wore a black padded bra.

"Her?" Tabby said. "Margaret. She's new. She's a friend of Liz's"

"Meg," I said. "They have me listed as Margaret . . ."

"Whatever," the girl said.

Tabby flipped her hair over her shoulder with a flick of the wrist. And then she and the skirts walked away.

* * *

I spent the weekend doing three things: going online to see if Tabby was online, ignoring Elizabeth's IMs inviting me to sleep over, and looking in the mirror as I practiced the way Tabby flipped her hair over her shoulder.

On Monday before homeroom, I saw Tabby getting her stuff out of her locker. The skirts were nowhere to be seen, so I walked up and said hi.

She was too busy fishing through her locker for something to say hi.

"I have something for you," I said.

She looked at me like I was interesting for the first time.

"What is it?"

"Meet me in the cloakroom," I said. "Before lunch."

"But Liz . . ."

I dangled my purse in the air between us, signaling that whatever I had was in there.

"Okay," she said. "Before lunch."

*   *   *

Elizabeth pounced on me as soon as Spanish was over. "Don't you know how to IM?" she said.

"Everybody knows how to IM," I said.

"Well, you didn't answer my messages," she said. "I invited you to sleep over."

"I know," I said. Then I flipped my hair over my shoulder just the way I'd practiced and walked off to meet Tabby in the cloakroom.

*   *   *

Except that she wasn't there. I waited for five minutes, then five more, then, just to be sure, five more. I was about to leave, planning to spend the rest of the lunch period in a bathroom stall in case she and Elizabeth came down after Tabby was done not eating, but just as I stepped into the skinny passageway I heard the faint squishing of rubber-soled footsteps coming in my direction. I ducked back into the cloakroom and flattened myself against the wall. I held my breath and listened. The footsteps stopped, then seemed to get quieter. Big Beef had evidently gone the other way.

*   *   *

Because of the Big Beef scare, I was late getting to math. Which meant the only seat left was next to Elizabeth. She smiled her Lego smile at me, then pointed to the open page in her textbook.

"We're on question number three," she whispered.

I barely nodded.

"You feeling okay?" she said. "You weren't at lunch."

I said I was fine.

Elizabeth studied my face.

"You sure?" she said. "You don't look okay."

I pretended I didn't hear her.

*　*　*

I saw Tabby at her locker at the end of the day. I put on my too-cool-to-be-bothered face as I walked past to go to my locker, but as soon as she turned around and looked in my direction, I said hi instead.

"What's up?" She said this like she completely forgot that we were supposed to meet in the cloakroom, like she completely forgot I had something for her.

"Nothing." I tried to sound casual.

She started walking away.

"I still have that, you know, that thing for you," I said.

"You have something for me?" she said from behind her curtain of hair. "Oh, yeah."

"Don't worry," I said, even though Tabby didn't exactly look worried. "It's no big deal."

As soon as I said it was no big deal, her eyes drifted off to someone or something else down the hall.

"Well," I said quickly. "It's sort of a big deal, I guess. I mean, it's . . . it's . . ." I tried to think of the right word. From the foggy look in Tabby's eyes I could tell she'd lost interest.

"It's unique," I said.

That got her attention. She checked her watch and said, "Okay, hurry up and give it to me. I have to be at my shrink's in twenty minutes."

I looked up and down the hall. "In the cloakroom," I said. "I can't show it to you here."

She blew on her bangs. "Okay," she said. "Just hurry up."

* * *

Being alone with Tabby in the cloakroom felt weird and different and not like I pictured it. Maybe it was because it was the end of the day, not lunchtime; maybe it was because it was just the two of us. Tabby blew on her bangs and looked bored, and for a minute I actually sort of wished Elizabeth was there with her Lego smile.

"So," said Tabby, "what is it?"

I reached inside my purse and pulled out a silver

monogrammed lighter. It was my mom's. She didn't smoke anymore, but she kept it in a velvet bag in her jewelry box.

I handed it to Tabby.

She regarded it absentmindedly. Her face was blank.

"So what do you think?" I said.

She shrugged. "It's okay."

"It's engraved." I turned it over so Tabby could see the big cursive letter *M* engraved on the front. "See? It's unique."

Tabby frowned. "It's not that unique. If it had more than one letter — like a person's monogram — that would be unique."

I tried to think of something to make it better. "It was in the family."

She shrugged. "So you want to have a smoke?"

"Sure."

She pulled out her cigarettes and shook the box up and down. "There's only one left," she said.

I had opened my mouth to say she could have it when Tabby handed it to me. "We can share," she said.

I tried not to beam the way Elizabeth did. Tabby Lane had said "we," meaning me and her.

While Tabby threw the empty cigarette box in the trash, I put the cigarette between my lips. Tabby gave the lighter an expert flick. The lid flipped open with a satisfying click, but nothing happened. Tabby frowned. I swallowed.

"Try again," I said.

On the second try it worked. I inhaled quickly before the flame went out. Which meant I inhaled the fumes from the lighter fluid as well as a big gulp of smoke. Which meant I coughed and choked until tears were streaming down my face. I looked up to see Tabby's reaction.

She was laughing. It was the kind of laugh where someone's laughing with you, not at you. I knew the difference, so I laughed, too.

Which only made me cough harder.

Tabby thumped me lightly on the back.

Which meant I was coughing and laughing at the same time.

"Margaret," came a deep voice from behind me. "Perhaps you'd like to tell me what's so funny."

I turned around and came face-to-face with Big Beef.

I looked at the cigarette in my hand, then at Tabby. Her ice-blue eyes were wide with fear.

I thought about dropping the cigarette on the floor and grinding it out with my heel, but that would add destruction of school property to the crime. So I just stood there holding the evidence.

Finally, Big Beef sighed. "Ms. Lane," said Big Beef. "Would *you* like to tell me what's going on?"

Tabby's face brightened a little. And my heart filled with gratitude toward my new friend, Tabby Lane, of *The* Lanes. She'd get us out of this.

She knocked one clog against the other while she thought of what to say.

Finally she looked up at Big Beef, tossed her hair so that it fell in that perfectly random, perfectly perfect way.

"Margaret's new," she said.

I nodded, innocent.

"She's a friend of Elizabeth's."

"I see," said Big Beef.

I didn't see. But I figured Tabby knew what she was doing.

I shifted the burning cigarette to my other hand. Ashes fell on the floor.

"Please, Mrs. Neville . . ." Tabby gave her an angelic smile. "Don't be mad."

I also gave her what I hoped was an angelic smile.

Mrs. Neville sighed. "Smoking is a very serious offense," she said. "*You* know that, Tabby."

"I know," Tabby said sadly. She bit her lip and looked out from under her bangs shyly. She was the picture of remorse, a blond-haired angel in a plaid skirt. She looked over at me and smiled sadly. Then she turned to Mrs. Neville. "She was just trying to fit in."

I didn't get it. Who was just trying to fit in? Elizabeth?

Mrs. Neville folded her arms across her chest. "That's no excuse."

Mrs. Neville looked me up and down, stopping a minute to take in the still-burning cigarette in my hand. Then she turned to stare at Tabby — who was holding her hands behind her back.

"Tabby," said Mrs. Neville. "What do you have behind your back?"

Tabby's eyes went wide again. "Nothing," she said in a small voice.

"Let me see, then," said Mrs. Neville.

Tabby brought one pale, skinny arm out from behind her back and wiggled her empty fingers. She smiled shyly.

"The other hand . . . ," said Mrs. Neville.

Tabby looked like she was about to cry. I pictured how when this was over, I'd try to cheer her up, how I'd put my arm around her frail little shoulders and tell her not to worry, that we'd have fun being suspended, that we could go to the mall or to her house and read magazines and listen to music while everyone else was in school.

Her wide blue eyes darted back and forth between me and Mrs. Neville.

Finally, she withdrew the hand behind her back. She opened her palm to reveal the silver lighter.

Mrs. Neville shook her head sadly.

Tabby shook her head sadly, too, then stepped toward Mrs. Neville. "Margaret tried to give this to me," she said. "See? It's engraved. With the letter *M.*"

I felt like I was falling, all of a sudden, even though I was standing up. When I looked over at the two of them, they seemed to be standing far away from me.

Mrs. Neville sighed heavily. "I see," she said.

And all at once I saw, too. But I stood there and waited for Tabby to make it crystal clear.

"See?" she said again, sidling up to Mrs. Neville. "It's unique."

SHASHIKALA: A BRIEF HISTORY OF LOVE AND KHADI
by Tanuja Desai Hidier

Varad, South Gujarat, Spring 1946

"LIGHT, OH, WHERE IS THE LIGHT?"

His eldest sister's voice coaxed him from his dream, singing a silken rip through the darkness. *"Kindle it with the burning fire of desire,"* she sang, her voice plaintive and urgent, as if it were the first human sound on earth. Anand could hear the scrape of mud and ash on the dishes, and the well bucket's creak as Zini Ben — Tiny Sister, so named for her hunchbacked three-foot stature — collected water for the day's needs. As was clear from the verse Zini Ben had chosen, by her beloved Tagore, the woodstove was certainly lit by now.

Anand snuggled deeper into the sheets, savoring the warmth from his wooden bed before he'd have to rise for school. Traces of his dream clung to him, and he closed his eyes, trying to catapult himself back into that world of possibility. In the dream he'd been gazing upon a tawny landscape and had shaped from its contours a nose — straight, with gently flared nostrils — full brown lips, and eyes so black they shone blue. It was Shashikala's face. Across it, like a beautiful broken dish, sat the beamed curve of a smile.

This smile was something his own fig-colored eyes had not seen upon her real eight-year-old face in the week since she'd moved in at the end of their row of houses. In the dream he had known, as awake he'd witnessed, that she had fine posture and took small, quick steps and knew special things. But in his sleep, she'd been happy and relaxed, the delicate red rims of her sad lids restored to their sandalwood hue. It had been a delicious dream, comforting as the surprisingly round belly of his slim mother when he was sick or afraid or missed his father, who'd been in South Africa for almost two years now.

Anand heaved himself onto his elbows. Poking out from under the pillow, he saw a corner of one of the dyed cotton flags his mother and Zini Ben had been working on in the evenings, with the narrow-waisted, wide-hipped women who met to make papad for their husbands' suppers. As of late, they'd been staying longer and longer and, once the papad had flickered and crisped in pans of oil and lay drying on the plate, they would turn their fingers to embroidering the orange, white, and green cloth rectangles. When the women left, Anand helped sew, as his brother, Deepak, used to, struggling to imitate his commanding script. This particular flag said *Bharat* across it — the ancient name for India. It was a freedom flag. An independence flag, meant to show that Anand and his fellow Indians would not be controlled anymore by the British. Some of the others said *Hind* or *Hindustan*, and had been slipped under other pillows and into rice containers since Betelnut Kaka — cousin Bulu's father, so named for the pleasure he took in chewing betelnuts, those icy kernels rolled in the thandak-spiked leaves — spread the word through the row of houses that the Bardoli officials were planning a village visit within the next week.

"Just to make sure things are under control, that we villagers aren't getting any ideas," Betelnut Kaka had snorted, his blackish teeth like gaps in his mouth. He'd lifted his chin, with its tuft of peppered beard, and added, "Imagine that! We villagers getting ideas!"

The village was Varad, in South Gujarat, a still, windless landscape set into motion only by the bullock carts, moving black and slow as mud, and the restless children who seemed to jostle the very sky as they skidded about, clouding the hot air with dust from the country lanes and roads. Anand's mother and Zini Ben rose at four, when the village mothers began their farming duties, tightening over the hours the knots of sound that by six o'clock brought the rows of linked homes entirely to life.

In Varad, families often built houses together, which were constructed to run into one another, four or five at a time. The houses were separated by doors that were usually left open, creating a labyrinth of aunts and uncles and in-laws and cousins. Parents often lost the ability to tell their children from the children of their siblings, as cousins exchanged places with cousins, or architecturally accumulated with them to triple their chapati intake in certain homes and halve the peace of mind of adults in others.

Within each house, the three living areas ran parallel to one another and out to the patio. Anand slept in the central room. Now, glancing at the other three beds, he saw that two were filled with the curled-up figures of his sleeping sisters, Urmila and Chandan. The third bed, Deepak's bed, was empty, as it had been for weeks, since he'd been sent to the private school in Bardoli. Anand's brother was no longer there, however: A week ago, word had come back through Uncle Betelnut that Deepak and six of his schoolmates had been taken to prison for setting fire to the town's police station. Evidence was mounting that this same clan — just days before — had removed the tiles from the train tracks running the Flying Rani cars south to Bombay.

"Be proud of your boy, Sister," Betelnut had said to Anand's distressed mother. "Yes, it's a bit of a stretch past *satyagraha*, but it's boys like these who will make the difference, bring cities to standstills, and force the officials — darker than us, some of them! — and their British gods to listen."

Satyagraha. Truth force. Anand had learned the word from his teacher, Mr. Patel, and had been hearing it nearly every day on the radio as well, in Gandhi's invocations for passive resistance to Great Britain's rule.

His mother's hands had dropped to his shoulders.

"He watched too many movies," she'd said.

* * *

Deepak got to have all the fun, Anand thought now. He wished he could be brave like his fiery-eyed big brother. *Then* Mr. Patel might notice him. *Then* Shashikala would smile upon him. The thought of her was like a piece of chocolate in his belly.

* * *

Anand recalled the evening before, when the smack of the twigs landing on the patio had caught his attention. He'd gone outside to give Durga, the Untouchable delivery woman, her payment of the day's leftover chapatis.

When he'd passed them to her, their hands had touched — just barely, but enough to warrant, were it made known, his having to be sprinkled with sanctifying water. Durga's eyes had flashed at him and she'd dipped her face down behind the rumpled curtain of her unbraided hair and scurried away. The contact had shot Anand through with a thrill that swelled to triumph when he did not tell the others and instead spent the evening rubbing Untouchability all over the house and into his sisters' hair — unbeknownst to them — with his unsanctified fingers.

When Deepak had lived at home, he had always gone out of his way to be the one to distribute their due to the members of this vilified caste; his fingers would graze the palms of the other, and he would maintain long moments of eye contact. He'd turned once to Anand, who always hovered nearby, in doorways and around corners, trying to soak up his brother's heroic climate.

"It starts here," he'd said, taking Anand's hand in both his own and clasping it, hard. "Do you see? It starts right here."

*　*　*

During the morning pooja, Anand prayed to be brave like Deepak one day and, finally, because he knew the last prayer was the strongest, he prayed for Shashikala.

"Keep her safe," he pleaded. "And make her happy and marry me. And don't forget about that buffalo cream."

In the kitchen, Zini Ben handed him a steel cup.

"*'What divine drink wouldst thou have, my God, from this overflowing cup of my life?'*" she quoted.

He looked down eagerly and then grinned at his half sister when he saw the beloved foam. The fragrance made it clear that she had crushed almonds into the milk. From her wan face a smile emerged, crooked and affectionate, and a little conspiratorial as well.

"*'This is my delight,'*" she said. "*'Thus to watch and wait at the wayside.'*"

Cup in hand, Anand joined the girls, cross-legged on the floor in the front room, and took his slate and newspaper-wrapped books from the satchel to write his ten tables. Today was to be a very important day in arithmetic class, the last spent on multiplication before the move on to division. The milk bubbled to his lips. He wondered whether Shashikala already knew everything they were teaching her at the girls' school; her haughty posture suggested that she'd probably covered the twenty tables by now. After all, he thought, as the soft scratch of his sisters' writing shivered the hairs of his neck, she was from Bombay — Powai Lake, actually, but that was close enough — and not only that; she was the prettiest girl he'd ever laid eyes upon, not at all like his sisters, who sat before him with the dull gleam of their delicate hunched bones and the long unwavering braids he was so often tempted to lop off with scissors as they lay sleeping. Shashikala's hair twisted thick to her shoulders, and he'd noticed — when his cousin Bulu and the others could not have noticed him noticing — that her arms were smooth and plump, and that she carried her books in them tidily all the way to school. She'd probably feasted on eye-watering curries, perhaps even dined on meat, a thought that both fascinated and disconcerted him, surrounded as he was by the village's lumbering buffalo and cows, the goats basking by the roadside with their slit pupils and slight smiles, and stray upon stray dog.

Shashikala was a cousin of a cousin of Anand's, which located her happily in the fourth of the adjoining homes, just past Bulu's. On the day she'd arrived, Anand had been at Bulu's, playing pirates on the swinging mosquito-netted beds, when they'd heard a low, sharp gasping. They'd followed the sound and, peeking through the door that joined Bulu's home to the next, saw her for the first time: Shashikala balled up against the wall, her head of loose inky hair burrowed into her knees. She'd snapped her face up to discover her audience and had fallen immediately silent, wiping her dripping nose across with her hand — until her hand looked as if it, too, had wept. Then she jumped up and dashed down farther into the maze of houses. Anand had been struck by her resemblance to someone, but he could not name who it was, where else the sparkling defiance of her expression, even in sadness, was to be found. Later, when he'd discovered she was from the warrior caste, Kshatriya — and not Vaishya, that of most of the farming villagers — he was even more surprised. He hadn't known that warriors could be found in the form of small, fierce girls, and crying, too.

"She sobs like the wind," Betelnut had confided to Anand's mother a few nights later. Anand had listened from the patio, where he'd been sucking the last bits of pulp from an aphoos mango peel. "And she paces. For hours through the night. Little footsteps and the *jing jing* of her anklet through the wall. It's as if the wall itself is singing! Singing and weeping all at once."

"It's terrible," Ba had said. "She must miss her parents, so far away in the city."

"She wanted to leave," said Betelnut. "She's angry with them, from what I understand."

"Whatever for?"

"A tragedy such as the one they've suffered! A child needs to lay the blame somewhere, I suppose."

"How young was he?" Ba had asked.

"I don't know. Fifteen. Sixteen."

"Deepak's age," she'd said.

There had been a silence, and then the shimmer of rice sifting through Ba's hands.

"Be thankful Deepak doesn't have a motorcycle," Betelnut had said, forcing a laugh.

"And what would he do with a motorcycle in prison?" Ba had snapped.

"Oh, Sister," Betelnut had sighed. "All I meant is, the girl's brother was on a motorcycle. It was an *accident*. This has nothing to do with Deepak."

"The boy was on his cycle," said Ba slowly. "He was delivering khadi bandages to the fighters the police beat down. The khadi was in his satchel — you told me yourself."

Betelnut had cleared his throat, then coughed, and said nothing.

"So you see," she'd said. "This has everything to do with Deepak."

* * *

"'*I ask for a moment's indulgence!*'"

Anand jumped at Zini Ben's quoting the children

77

back to the kitchen. It was already past ten, and he wolfed down dripping fingerfuls of chapatis and buttermilk soup. His sisters finished the midday meal before he did and went to meet their friends down the lane. Anand was rising to go when Zini Ben crossed him with an arm.

"Aaray, wait, Anand," she said. "Let them go on. Ba has something for you."

He saw his mother then, through the doorway. She emerged from the shadows of the central room with the sweeping pallor of a ghost, swathed as she was in a white cotton sari, glasses turned to impenetrable discs of light. She rippled toward them, as if moving through great heat or wind, as if on the verge of coming apart altogether. Her arms were piled high with the soft flags she and Zini Ben had spun together and khadi bandages.

These days, everything in the house was made of khadi — homespun cotton. Weeks before, they'd met with some of the other villagers at twilight and held a bonfire in the field. The burning smell of his old clothes and those of the other children and aunts and uncles sifted to the sky, which blinked in the sputtering light. Anand had been amazed at his mother that night: Her high, wide forehead, which was lined across like writing paper when she dug through her rupee box, was smooth as on the days his father's envelope arrived with the Johannesburg stamps that Anand saved in matchboxes. Ba's eyes had been invisible, and flames had darted in her thin framed glasses; her mouth was set and untwitching in its beaklike pursing as she dropped first a pair of dungarees, then a frock, into the lunging fire.

"From now on we will wear nothing made in Liverpool or Birmingham," she told the children that evening, unbundling the fresh white khadi clothing she and Zini Ben had been spinning for weeks. Among them were the snug Gandhi caps the boys wore from that day on to school. "No linen, no poplin. We grow the cotton, and we will grow the clothes as well."

Now the floorboards creaked like bones beneath Ba's feet, and the hem of her sari danced around her chappals. As she approached Anand, her face drew in color, as if from the surroundings. The room dimmed and her skin grew gold. She gestured to him to give her his satchel. From it, she drew one of his textbooks — a huge battered volume of history, which had been handed down to him by Deepak — and carefully layered the cotton cloths between book and cover, smoothing them down with her rough palms until the book hardly seemed padded at all.

"This is your new history book," Ba said. Then she

cupped Anand's chin and bent her own head down till the tip of her birdlike nose grazed that of his ball-like one.

"Son," she said in a voice that made him stand up straighter. "Give these at the end of the day to Mr. Patel *only*. Not to Mr. Bhatya, not to Mr. Raga. Mr. *Patel* is expecting these. If there are police on the road, you are only carrying your schoolbooks. Nothing is different. Now go and don't be late. Go to school."

Anand's mouth puckered into an astonished *O!* as he put his book back into the satchel. Ba watched him with a frightening intensity, and he saw that Zini Ben was watching, too, her eyes full of sorrow and tenderness.

He panicked, felt he had to hurry and, hugging bag to chest and pushing cap to head, turned to dash through the row of houses — shouting out *good mornings* and *namaste*s to the uncles and aunts swinging on hitchkas or crouched sifting rice — through the first and second and at last to the third doorway, where Bulu stood, exhibiting the naturally taunting expression he was blessed with due to the pairing of his upraised brows and heavy-lidded eyes.

"You're late!" Bulu said, accusingly. "Now we'll never chase her."

Shashikala, Anand thought. *That* was why he'd felt

so pressed. The thought of her made him feel soft and good, like the pistachio kulfi ice cream he got to eat on holidays.

"No, *you're* late!" cried Anand, and pushed past Bulu through the front door. Outside, the day blared sunshine, dispelling the fears Anand had felt in shadow. "Now let's see who's the rotten egg!"

* * *

The walk to school was really no more than a five-minute one, but the children took at least twenty to get there, traveling through their various rows of joined homes to collect their cousins, then down the tree-lined lanes to the main road, where little by little their groups accumulated members filing in from other lanes, until two bands of children marched among the bullock carts: frocked girls with linked arms and long shining braids, and boys shuffling pebbles, pretending not to watch them.

Today Chandan and Urmila and the two girls they walked with, all skinny and drifting in pale loose-fitting dresses, were already so far down the lane their soft voices were tramped out by the boys' footsteps. Anand watched as the dust puffed up around his chappaled feet, as if the earth were exhaling. He felt the bite of the satchel strap on his shoulder.

"We could always chase them," said Bulu, a little glumly.

"Who?" said Anand.

"Them. The girls."

"I suppose," said Anand, stooping to pick up a rock. He noted curiously that, though he was no longer moving, dust still clouded his toes, as if stirred by a tiny scarce wind. He was certainly going to be dirty by the time he got to school, he thought, aiming and firing at a well-laden branch of a tamarind tree.

"Wait," said Bulu.

"What?"

Bulu lowered his voice.

"She's behind us."

"Who?"

"Shh! Shashikala — no, don't look!"

"How do you know?"

"I just know, that's all."

"You *looked*," whispered Anand, feeling both superior for not looking and a little irritated that he had not noticed first.

Anand slowed down his pace. He could hear a jingle and saw a peripheral dash of color and then the small quick-stepped red-robed figure of Shashikala. Her anklet's refrain grew louder with her approach.

"You're right," Anand admitted.

"I told you not to look."

"I didn't," he said. "Just like you."

"Well," said Bulu. "We could always chase her."

"Fool," said Anand. "How are we supposed to chase her? She's behind us."

"If we slow down she'll get ahead. And you should have no trouble doing *that,* slowpoke that you are."

Both of them fell silent, chewing nervously on their tamarind seeds. Neither slowed down. Anand wondered whether Bulu could hear his heart whip against his chest. The patter of approaching footsteps made them both jerk their heads to the side, where Shashikala was passing, hair skidding down the nape of her neck, dust reeling away from the magical red dress. She stared straight ahead and was blinking very quickly.

Anand's heart rose to his mouth and his brows twinkled with sweat. Ahead, he could see his sisters with their girlfriends.

"Or we could always chase Chandan," Bulu offered.

"Yes!" cried Anand. "Yes, let's!"

A weight was lifted from him, and he saw that his cousin looked relieved as well.

"*AHH!*" Bulu cried. "They're the messengers; we're the police!" And the two bounded toward the girls, who glanced one by one over their shoulders, saw the out-stretched boy hands, and turned, shrieking away in terror, their braids slapping, suddenly alert, against the smalls of their backs.

The boys let the girls stay just meters ahead, in order to prolong their agony. They did not let up until they arrived at the one-story four-room schoolhouse and the girls split off for their school a bit farther across the field, which stretched on beyond the two buildings. In the boys' play yard, a round of kabaddi was taking place, the game in which each team tried to tag all the members of the other team while calling out, "*Kabaddi! Kabaddi! Kabaddi!*" — as many times as possible in one breath.

Shashikala, Shashikala, Shashikala, Anand thought as he dashed madly through the dirt, encumbered today by the satchel he refused to let lie.

"*Kabaddi!*" he shouted.

*   *   *

When the bell clanged, the boys collected their fallen caps and lined up grade by grade with the four teachers to sing the national anthem. Across the field, the girls were doing the same. Anand strained to draw Shashikala from the crowd, but his view was curtailed by the higher heads of the third- and fourth formers.

Mr. Surat Bhatya, the headmaster, stood to the side, stuffed into his pale blue linen suit. His umbrella was popped open to shield his head — pith helmeted as it already was — from the sun's skin-darkening rays. He had the virescent pallor of a dazzlingly unripe fruit and his cheeks puffed and unpuffed with his breathing, but he did not sing.

Under Anand's breath, the prayer to the motherland today became a love song for Shashikala.

*   *   *

After arm stretches and toe touches, they separated. Anand entered the second-form classroom with his cousin and eleven other boys, where they sat on the floor in ranking order. From his own seat, in the middle of the sea of students, Anand envied the rest of them. He wished he could be singled out in some way, be at least brave, if not so smart. That way Shashikala would surely marry him, one day, when he would be old enough to talk to her.

Deepak, like Bulu, had been a last-rower and had always been so courageous — sneaking cigarettes behind the tamarind trees and even daring to talk back, telling the teachers that he did not need to learn in school what the world would surely teach him.

"Then go to the world," Ba had finally said, angrily, but her hawklike eyes were fierce with love. "Go learn something."

And that is how Deepak had ended up in Bardoli in the first place, sent to a private school for the ill-disciplined, where the students had to wash their own clothes and cook, too. There he had befriended the group of similarly ill-disciplined but energetic boys who kept their eyes on the streets, where history seemed these days to be written, rather than in the books, where the printed words would not sway, at best would fade.

Today Mr. Patel seemed distracted, his cheeks swollen purple, as if he'd been pinching them all morning. His sooty hair sprouted in kinetic disarray from his head and his eyes were two bolts of light, relentless over the baggy folds around them. Lately the eyes of all the village elders were turning into these bolts, Anand realized, recalling Ba's and Zini Ben's faces that morning.

"Namaste, class," Mr. Patel said. He had chipped teeth. Sometimes when he spoke his tongue flecked into the cracks and led his voice along a lisping curl that usually made Anand giggle. Mr. Patel paced the floor in his dusty chappals. When he stood still, his toes curled up and down, up and down, but out of sync as if they were flailing for grounding.

"Today is an important day," Mr. Patel continued, and Anand thought he saw his eyes rest upon him for a moment. He squirmed, trying to recall whether he'd forgotten to do any of his lessons or was dustier than usual. Before he could arrive at a third idea — which, he was beginning to think, might involve his history book and what it hid — Chothu had begun the reading exercises.

* * *

During recess, the boys broke up to play hide-and-seek. Anand was It and chose the far mango tree by which to count. He turned away from his scattering classmates and looked to the girls' field. In the distance he could see her, a splotch of color bleeding against the dull backdrop, like a small rip in the universe. She sat apart from the other girls, who linked arms to bump the ring-around-the-rosy. Shashikala's back was to them, her hands dancing light upon something in her lap. Then, sharply, she drew her right hand back, high as her shoulder, and dropped it again to her lap. She rolled her palm gently outward and drew it back again, as if caressing the bow of some invisible instrument.

Anand overcounted, lost track, started over. He wondered what Shashikala's secret gestures meant, what she could possibly be thinking about. It was hard to tell from her face, impervious as it usually was except for the dusky shadows of exhaustion around her eyes. Perhaps her mind was occupied with Bombay, with its laneless traffic and glittering marketplaces and the arched Gateway opening its yellow arms to the scorched cinnamon sea that had ushered in the British so many years ago. Perhaps her thoughts were held by that sixteen-year-old boy who had had the accident, that stranger Anand felt he knew, who made him long for his brother and for his father and to do something to help. If only he could speak to Shashikala, what amazing things would she tell him?

* * *

"You are truly pretty," he would say. "Like Sita in the Garden of Asoka, and even Ba in the pictures when she married Bapuji."

"Thank you," Shashikala would say.

"Maybe we can sit under the mango tree together," he would say. "I won't pull your hair."

"You are truly brave," she would say. "Just like your brother, but braver."

And he would see her smile.

* * *

Now Shashikala sat still, her hands folded in her lap, her gaze fixed upward and ahead. Anand turned away. His classmates were nowhere to be seen. By the schoolhouse door, Mr. Patel stood, head bouncing fervently. One hand was hooked under his cap and into his hair, the other sunk and twitching in his pants pocket. He was standing with Mr. Nair and listening to the village elders — Rakeshji and Romilji — whose arrival Anand had not noticed and whose presence was odd, especially at midday. Their white pants billowed from their ankles in a still more peculiar slight breeze. When Rakeshji finished speaking, all four of them smiled and nodded.

A quick movement inside the schoolhouse veered Anand's attention to the window just to the side of the four men. This was the window of the headmaster's office, and through it Anand thought he caught a glimpse of the bowl of Mr. Bhatya's infamous pipe, clutched in a trembling hand. Anand was wondering how long the headmaster had been standing there listening, why he did not join in, when Mr. Nair rang the bell that signaled the end of recess.

As if by magic, scores of small boys began to emerge, dropping down tree trunks and sliding around corners and out from the folds of the earth.

"Slowpoke, Anand!" one cried out.

"Spoilsport!" claimed another. "You didn't even try."

"I lost track counting," said Anand as they lined up to go back inside for arithmetic.

"Liar! How could you lose track counting?"

"He was staring at the girls!" Pulau piped up.

"I was not staring at them!"

"He was! He was! There, you see? Girl looker! Girl looker!"

"You have pointy ears!" Anand cried out, to no one in particular, as the boys jostled their way back into the classroom. "And you're not brave like me!"

"What's brave about you?" someone challenged just as Mr. Patel entered the room. "Your brother's the brave one."

Anand's eyes smarted as he sat down. He wished he could erase what he'd heard as easily as the chalk from the slate he placed now in his lap.

* * *

When the final bell rang at five o'clock, Anand turned to Bulu.

"Wait for me," he said.

"I'll wait outside," his cousin said. "I want to kick a rock at Pulau."

Pulau had accidentally hit Bulu with a pebble during kabaddi the day before.

When the classroom emptied out, Anand stood, satchel in arms. Mr. Patel's back was to him as he wiped down the blackboard. Anand stepped forward and cleared his throat.

"Mr. Patel?" he ventured.

Mr. Patel turned. He put the eraser down.

"Anand," he said.

Anand fumbled nervously though his bag. He felt strange being alone with the teacher, as if he had broken a very important rule or, even more awkward, as if the two of them were breaking a rule together.

"Here," Anand said at last, presenting him with the carefully wrapped textbook and its hidden cloths. "They're inside."

Mr. Patel nodded very seriously, and was unwrapping the paper when they were startled by a familiar voice.

"Good day, Pruthub."

It was Mr. Bhatya, the headmaster. He filled up the doorway with his hefty figure, as if blocking their escape. From his lips the pipe dangled, pulling the corner of his mouth down into a frown. With one hand he gripped his briefcase, with the other, the handle of the now-folded umbrella, which he tapped briskly on the floor, shattering the silence that followed his greeting.

Mr. Patel's hands froze momentarily on the book.

Then, without further hesitation, he packed it into his own cotton bag, followed by a folder and the tin in which he carried his chapatis.

"Hello, Surat," he said evenly.

"And what is happening here?" said Mr. Bhatya, sliding the umbrella into the crook of his arm and taking the pipe from his lips. Smoke clouded his eyes.

"Well, Surat," said Mr. Patel, and Anand was amazed to see how neatly and nearly imperceptibly two thin windows pushed down over his pupils, fogging them at a first glance into a dull, uncomprehending state. "Nothing much. Just packing up to go home. What do you suppose would be happening?"

"Just a friendly question, Pruthub. Making conversation. Nothing wrong with making a little conversation, is there, now?" After a pause, he slowly added, "Bloody shame about the Karnik girl's brother, isn't it?"

"It's a tragedy," said Mr. Patel.

"Better to remain peaceful, wouldn't you say?"

Mr. Bhatya turned to Anand. "Any word from your brother?" he asked. He seemed to be smiling.

Anand's head throbbed and he looked down.

"Yes, just as I suspected," said Mr. Bhatya, sounding triumphant. He turned back to Mr. Patel. "A bloody shame indeed. If only the boy hadn't been defying authority. And the girl seems to be a bit of a trouble-maker herself."

"If only the authorities hadn't *thrashed* all those young boys with their canes," said Mr. Patel. His lip trembled and he sank his teeth into it. His eyes sparked, just a bit. "All they were doing was demonstrating. Peacefully."

"No demonstration is peaceful," said Mr. Bhatya. "Let's not kid ourselves, Pruthub. And we all know what a little demonstration can lead to."

With his left hand, Mr. Patel began to sweep eraser shavings, one by one, from the desktop and into his right hand. It was the only sound in the tensely silent space.

"Well then," said Mr. Bhatya, and his jowls puffed and deflated with his quick breathing. "I trust I will see you tomorrow?"

The room seemed too small to contain them.

"Tomorrow," said Mr. Patel. "You will certainly see me."

He picked up another folder from the desk.

"You can go now," he said. It was unclear whether the utterance was directed at Anand or Mr. Bhatya.

But Anand didn't wait to find out. He rushed out of the musty building and into the searing playground sunlight.

*　*　*

"Slowpoke!" grumbled Bulu, who was leaning against the mango tree. His feet were ringed with the matches he'd no doubt been delighting in lighting in such proximity to the teachers.

"*You're* the slowpoke!" cried Anand. Now, outside, his fear turned to spirit and energy. He began to run, out of the school yard and onto the main road. "I'm the messenger! You're the police!"

Dust swirled up from his feet and rose to cloud him to the waist so that he seemed to be skimming a sea of fog. Bulu's panting grew louder, creating hot patches on the back of Anand's neck, and his nearing footsteps doubled the density of the dust floating around their whirring legs. The road was empty now except for mango peels and tamarind seeds and the frayed ribbons of some unlucky girl whose hair had been successfully pulled down. And for a few moments, Anand was the messenger — just like Deepak and Betelnut Kaka, the young boys and hopeful men who walked miles on foot from city to town to village, beginning the whisper through the joined rows of houses of the latest developments in the cities, and who returned from village to town to city, distributing homespun bandages and news of the solidarity of even these remote regions of the country with the others. In the midst of these thoughts, Bulu tagged his elbow.

"Enough," said Bulu. "I caught you. Now *you're* the police."

"No!" said Anand, and he felt he might cry. "I will never be the police. *Never!*"

"What's the matter? It's just a game."

"It's not a game," said Anand. "Something exciting is going on; I can tell."

They were turning onto the lane home. Anand was considering his options when Bulu slammed a hand on his shoulder and slowed him down.

"Oh Ram, there she is," Bulu whispered. "Why is she so late going home, too?"

Ahead of them was the red-dressed, perfectly erect little figure, flowing forward with the measured grace of a small dancer.

"You want excitement?" said Bulu. "Then chase her!"

"Why don't *you* chase her?"

"I'm not the one who said anything about excitement," said Bulu. "Besides, I dare you. What are you afraid of, anyway? All she'll do is run away. She's a girl."

When Anand didn't say anything, Bulu added: "Deepak would have done it."

Before the terrifying prospect of being so close to Shashikala could fully register, Anand's feet leaped up like tiny fish, and he was running, so hard, so breathlessly fast, he felt his legs had spun out of their casings and turned to wheels.

The red image grew brighter. Shashikala whipped her head around and turned to face the boy: the flushed lips, the indignantly flared nose; the black eyes grew bluer and bluer, seemed to push the dust away with their disorienting color, taking up as much space as possible, until Anand was so close to her — she who did not run — that he had no choice but to stop running. This he did, and stayed there, hopping a little foolishly from one foot to the other, not quite knowing what to do in this unforeseen situation, as Shashikala, her fists pushed into her slight hips, regarded him evenly and with complete composure.

Anand was stunned. He was so near that, were he to suffer a bout of insanity, he could have reached out with his toe to touch the anklet jingling upon her slender chappaled foot. His dream swooped upon him again and his eyes lovingly traced her features. She did not smile, and Anand realized at that moment why she looked so familiar: Her eyes shone with the fierce light that Zini Ben and Ba had sometimes, that Mr. Patel had today and Uncle Betelnut whenever he returned from the towns and cities. The light that scalded Bulu's eyes and that perpetually inhabited those of Deepak, like beacons in two windows; even Durga the Untouchable had had something of this. Anand felt he'd hit upon a truth, nameless and brief but sure as the hands of his mother on the wheel, the quiet shimmer on the muscled backs of the bullocks; he felt the perfect *O!* of his mouth pop into position as Shashikala turned and continued down the lane, neither more slowly nor more quickly than before. He froze, felt Bulu's breathing on his neck. When she was just a blot of red, a blurred distant heart, she vanished into her home.

*   *   *

That night in Varad a wind rose that was unusual and quite bold. It shook up the dust in the yards, creaked the windows, and filtered through from house to house, everywhere setting the mosquito-netted beds swinging, as if ghosts had awakened from a long slumber and begun to move about and stretch their bones.

Anand was sitting with his sisters, who were trying to be stoic, true village girls, but gave away their terror nevertheless with shifty-eyed glances at all the new flutterings of the house. The children were on the floor, slates upon their laps, though none of them had written a single word but sat, chalk in hands, hands flitting above the dark surfaces, as if they were unsure of what words to say or in what language to say them. Ba and Zini Ben bent over trying to weigh down the spinning wheels that, charged with the frenzied air, thrashed back against them. The thread was whirling out of control, unraveling what had been done, setting the wheels into motion as if drawn on the cart of some speedy god.

Zini Ben curved her whole small body over the wheel and lay there clinging to it; she seemed on the verge of spinning off herself.

"*'Art thou abroad on this stormy night on thy journey of love, my friend?'*" she whispered.

Like a heavy knuckle, a blast of wind crashed against the house, and the door joining Anand's home to the next flew open. In it stood a very flustered-looking Betelnut Kaka, still in traveling shoes and a white jacket dusted to beige, wind-adorned with bits of grass and twigs and pistachio shells.

"Tomorrow!" he cried, and flung his arms open. "There will be no school! Our village will finally join in! No school! We will meet under the sun."

Zini Ben gasped rapturously and clambered down

from the wheel to let it spin, its whirring adding a harmony to the wind's song.

"At last," she said. "The long night of our despair breaks its fists into day."

"Now," said Betelnut, brushing off his lapels. "I don't believe I've ever read that poem."

"That's just me," Zini Ben said, and smiled. "That's my own voice."

No school. Anand shivered excitedly. *We will meet under the sun.*

* * *

That night, he lay awake for hours, and when at last he hurled off his waking ledge, he turned into a bird, brilliant and red breasted, and zoomed in and out of tunnels that were the pupils of eyes, and these eyes, he noted in a final epiphany, were the eyes of his mother and of Zini Ben, of Mr. Patel and even Mr. Nair. Of the Untouchable, of Bulu and his father. Of Deepak and of Shashikala.

* * *

In the morning the wind had not died down at all. If anything, it had increased. In fact, it was not Zini Ben's voice that awoke Anand but the gust that burst in through the window and tore the sheets from him and off the huddled bodies of his sisters, so that being in this room of white billowing and curled-under air currents must have been, Anand imagined, very much like being inside a wave.

The children worked their way through the house, merrily ducking under and dodging the cotton cloths and dresses and fragments of papad, and the hundreds of letters from their father in South Africa, which were floating everywhere, as if lifted upon water. Anand and his sisters gathered around the fire to clean their teeth, and the wind wracked the stove and the trees so that jackfruit thudded of its own accord into the baskets Ba had had the foresight to place strategically on the patio, and the flames snaked up and flared, like cobras from charmers' baskets. Today, none of this was frightening. When first one and then another acacia twig flew from the corner of Urmila's mouth, Anand felt building inside him a giddiness that was unshackled when she and then Chandan and he and even the two older women broke into delighted squeals.

*　　*　　*

The walk from the lanes to the road and then down the road was markedly different today. Anand and Bulu stayed close to their sisters, trying to clear themselves a breathing space in the frenetically stirred dust. It was difficult to see — which made it impossible for Anand to look for Shashikala, although he was a bit embarrassed to, anyway, after the events of the day before — and they had to take great care of their heads, for caps were flying and fruit was falling, punctuating the morning with the bang of mangos and the fuzzy tumble of tamarinds. Blue ribbons unknotted from the hair of the girls and flew like snips of sky past the accumulating band of children.

Then, by some unspoken accord, all the girls and boys began to run, fast, then faster, as if they, like the weather, could not contain themselves. The two buildings approached — the girls' school on the left, the boys' on the right, in front of which a nearly maroon Mr. Bhatya stood, waving fist and umbrella in the air — but the children ran right past, the hair of all the girls now undone and rippling like dark wheat behind them. They skidded through the designated play areas and out, at last, into the open fields.

Anand excitedly scanned the scene. In the shade of the mango trees stood Mr. Patel and Mr. Nair and Rakeshji and Romilji — the elders Anand had seen the day before — all wildly unkempt and beckoning the children in. A stone's throw away, but with no walls separating them this time, the women who taught at the other school were standing open armed, drawing in the girls as well.

As he walked toward the men, Anand heard a high-pitched wail:

"Wait! You must study! You must go to school! School must go on!"

Anand glanced back over his shoulder. From this vantage point, beyond the schools, Mr. Bhatya looked so inconsequential, a floundering speck in a storm. His umbrella had snapped inside out, and he bobbed up and down as he jerked in the air, so that he seemed, comically, to be trying to contain all the sun and wind of the world in its scaled shredding cup. The wind knocked his pith helmet from his head and, for the first time, Anand saw that Mr. Bhatya was indisputably and completely bald.

Anand was amazed at the headmaster's transformation. Just yesterday, this same man had with complete confidence and lack of sensitivity called Deepak into question and Shashikala, too. Anand turned away from the schoolhouse and strained his eyes to find the one, that precious one, Mr. Bhatya had dared to call a troublemaker.

In a matter of moments, Anand discovered her. Under the mango tree closest to the boys' area sat Shashikala, in lotus position against the trunk. Her red dress fanned flutteringly across her lap and she stared upward and ahead, the way she'd been staring yesterday at recess, her ink-black hair tossing itself round the tree trunk. Today, however, Anand noticed, many of the girls sat like her, upright and pleased, some attempting to rebraid each other's hair, others not bothering at all.

"Good morning, boys and girls!" Mr. Patel called, stepping out of the shade. "As you can see, today is a very special day for all of us. And so, before we begin, I would like to give you all a little something. But first I need two very *ssspecial* students to assist me."

Ahead of him, Anand saw Chothu puff up his shoulders a bit, preparing to rise, and Pulau's hand trembled into his disheveled hair as he tried in vain to smooth it.

"Shashikala," said Mr. Patel. "And Anand."

For a moment, Anand experienced a separation of word from thing; he could hardly allow himself the divine pleasure of thinking that *he* was the Anand being addressed, and in the same breath as Shashikala as well, though he hoped with all his heart he was. But when he looked up, shy and confused, he saw that the eyes of Mr. Patel — who seemed transformed this morning, neither distracted nor flushed — were intent on Anand's and Anand's alone, taking him in with an unprecedented lucidity.

Mrs. Pani went to Mr. Patel, then, and focused a similar gaze upon Shashikala, who stood, a wind-swayed rose in her perpetual red dress. When she began to walk, Anand did as well, to the very front, where they took their places between the two teachers. Once again he was in Shashikala's proximity and, not only that, but also, for the first time in his life, singled out before all the children, and even adults. He remained strangely calm, and a quiet, intense joy flowed through him.

"Shashikala stayed late at school with me," announced Mrs. Pani in her high-pitched voice, "and spent her recess periods helping to sew and stitch the khadi bandages that will go on to the cities and towns, and hopefully ease the pains of the many freedom fighters there. Her brother was one of them, as some of you know, and we still deeply grieve his loss."

Anand started. From the corner of his eye, he saw that Shashikala continued to stare straight ahead. However, here, before a whole group of people, the look was fitting. She *belonged* here. And Anand? He couldn't imagine how he had ended up beside her.

"Anand," Mr. Patel shouted over the wind, and Anand shivered with delight at the realization that, yes, Mr. Patel was talking about him. "Anand brought independence flags to the schoolhouse, some of which have already gone on to Bombay and other towns. He carried them with courage through the lanes and the roads, despite the fact that the police have been expected for days now. And I have some here with me today, to pass out for you to wear. Just one moment."

Mr. Patel had pulled from his bag the old history text and was beginning to peel away the newspaper cover when a particularly strong gust of wind blew the book up from his hands, tearing the paper all the way off. His hair shrieked outward, and he leaped up to catch the flung-open book, clamped down on and held it open with one hand on each now-exposed cover.

"Oh my!" he cried, in delight. "Oh my!"

For the wind had dug so fiercely into the history book's binding that all the pages came undone and mingled with the already air-bound flags until the sky seemed to be composed entirely of white and green and orange wings and the waving brown hands of jumping children.

Red flashed in Anand's peripheral vision and he turned to see Shashikala leaping to catch hold of a passing flag. She pulled it down and smoothed the orange and green and white across her chest and looked at him; her eyes had turned entirely blue and were flickering. He was nervous for a moment that she was perhaps still angry about yesterday's chase and that the flag would fly from her hands as she moved to plunge them back into her hips, when he heard her quiet voice.

"Anand," she said, "you are truly brave."

He jerked up his head to look at her. She had pinned the flag, which said *Bharat,* in the crooked uneven scrawl he knew so well and had tried so hard to change, to the front of her dress. She was smiling.

THE WILD PRINCE
by Brian Selznick

THIS IS MY BACKYARD. Over there is the hill where everyone goes sledding in the winter, and over there is the small yellow bush, and over there is the big tree that I now know is going to die in a few years and fall down. The tree will slowly rot away until the only thing left of it is this memory and the words written across the paper you are now touching, which was, of course, made from some other tree that someone else, somewhere, might be remembering right now. And over there, if you squint because the sun is in your eyes, is the huge rumbling air-conditioning unit that cools the entire house. Come and take a closer look with me. The ground here is muddy and covered in weeds, and when I first moved into this house I played here in the dirt.

Kneel down in the weeds here. This is exactly where I was when I found him. I was kneeling, just like you are now, digging and playing, when I made a most incredible discovery. I thought at first he was a twig or a strange little rock, but I pulled him out of the grass and looked at him lying there in the palm of my hand. I had discovered a tin soldier, the way others before me had discovered Egyptian tombs and sunken ocean liners. Who had left this soldier behind? What kid had forgotten him? The soldier was covered in dirt, and he immediately became my treasure. I washed him carefully and examined him closely. His red-painted uniform was faded and scratched, and there was still a hint of a black mustache on his tiny face. His outstretched hand was empty. I turned him over and saw that the letters *WP* were stamped into his base. His tin hat had faded, and he wore some kind of backpack that I figured had once been black and gray.

I brought him everywhere with me, keeping him hidden in my pocket. Sometimes at night I would stare at him, hoping he would reveal something to me about his past, but he stood steadfast and silent. This mystery made me feel dizzy sometimes, and I loved him. I did drawings for him, pictures of battles that I thought he might like, and I imagined his friends, all thinking him lost, wishing he were with them again so they could tell stories about the past and laugh and sing. I imagined my soldier had sacrificed himself for the others, so they could escape. I was sure my soldier was a hero and a true friend. He had to be brave to be outside in the tall weeds by himself for so long, never moving, never shivering, never crying. Even as his paint faded and his gun was lost, he didn't lose faith. Maybe he knew that I'd find him one day. Why be scared when you know you are going to be saved? I imagined the rain falling on him, and the snow, and the bugs crawling over him. And still he didn't move. Had he been there for weeks? Months? Years? How long had he waited for me to show up? How had he known I would come? I didn't know, but I was glad he waited. I'd never saved anyone before, and the responsibility was huge.

Now look over there, on the other side of my yard, past the small yellow bush, and you'll see the edge of a forest that divides our property from the new development going up across the way. I was afraid my soldier wouldn't like being cooped up in my pocket all day, so I built him a castle. I spent hours and hours building bridges and turrets and tunnels that snaked in and out of the ever-growing fortress of twigs at the edge of this forest. A miniature world rose here, all for my single, lonely, faded soldier, who had nothing in the world except me.

* * *

I think Ezra noticed me first at school. I was sitting at the back of the class, feeling like I couldn't stand another minute without looking at my soldier, so I pulled him out of my pocket. I covered him with my palm and brought him to my desk. I opened my fingers like a bowl and looked at him hidden in my shaking hands.

That's when Ezra noticed me. He had never said anything before to me, but I had seen him writing at the desk next to mine. His face was usually a little dirty and his hair was never cut well. I had never seen him smile and, to tell you the truth, he scared me a little. Since my mother cut my hair, I figured his mother cut his hair, too. His clothes were messy. So were mine.

But something happened when he saw me looking at my soldier. Ezra smiled. And I knew right away I could trust him. Isn't that odd? It happened that fast. I angled my hands toward him and he became, at that moment, the only other person in the entire world who knew about my soldier.

Later that day, I told him the stories I had made up about my soldier, his heroism, his bravery, and then Ezra began to write stories about my soldier himself. I pointed out the letters *WP* and, without hesitating, he said they stood for *Wild Prince*, and that this soldier was a prince who had to run away in disguise. No one knew he was really a prince who had been raised by wolves.

Ezra started writing the stories down and he read them to me on the playground, and I was happy. I invited him to my house. I showed him the unfinished castle at the edge of the forest. He didn't say a word. He just reached down and began working on it, as if he'd always been here.

*   *   *

Ezra came to me one morning at school and told me he had begun to have dreams about my soldier. At first I didn't believe him. I thought it was another story. But he looked serious. He said it was always the same strange dream. In the dream, my soldier was missing. Ezra saw me get up and look out my window. There, below me, running across the lawn, was my soldier heading toward the forest. The soldier was lit by the silver globe of the moon, and his inky shadow was following him right along. In the dream, I opened my window and called to him. I called after the Wild Prince, but he didn't turn around. He just kept running, sometimes on all fours like a wolf, until he had disappeared completely into the blackness of the forest.

Ezra said he usually woke up at this moment, sweating and scared.

I believed him. I took the soldier out of my pocket and handed him to Ezra.

"Here," I said. "Why don't you take him home tonight?"

* * *

I knew he would take good care of the soldier, and I wanted him to have the Wild Prince for the night. It was the first time the soldier would be away from me, but I knew he'd be safe with Ezra.

* * *

The next day we discovered that we had both had the same dream the night before. We both saw the soldier running once again, sometimes on all fours, into the forest. We got goose bumps when we said it. And we knew what we had to do.

* * *

So this is the exact spot where Ezra and I first stepped into the forest. We weren't scared, because we were with each other, and our soldier. I knew I wasn't supposed to go into the forest. My parents had told me very clearly. I had never disobeyed a rule like this before. I knew the difference between right and wrong, but now, for the first time in my life, I was sure I was right, even though I'd been told it was wrong. I had to go. *We* had to go.

The crunching sounds of the twigs and dried leaves beneath our feet echoed in our ears, and it's a sound that I love to this day. The air changed and became green.

Here and there, bright shafts of light penetrated the leafy ceiling, and burst down through the air, hitting the ground like spotlights on glowing leaves. Everything moved and was alive. I held the soldier so his head was free to look out on this world, on the adventure he was leading us into. Ezra and I didn't know what we would find, but somehow we were sure we would find something beyond the trees and leaves and birds and twigs.

And we were right.

*　*　*

At first it seemed like a mirage, because what we were seeing seemed impossible. But we were both seeing it at the same time. There, rising in the center of the forest, was an abandoned building. Its windows and most of its walls had long ago fallen away, so what was left looked like lace. The forest snaked through it and grew so completely that the branches and vines of the forest looked like they were holding up the building. Most amazingly of all, there was a sign sitting crooked on the roof, two huge metal letters that were now home to hundreds of birds and squirrels. The two letters were *WP*! Our soldier's letters! The Wild Prince! What was going on?

I looked down and kicked aside some of the leaves. I saw that the ground was covered in what I first thought was dozens, then I realized was hundreds and thousands, of tin soldiers. I poked Ezra and pointed downward. A vast sea of soldiers blanketed the ground. At first they blended into their surroundings, like good camouflage, but once your eyes adjusted you began to see the bits of red and black that could only belong to more soldiers. We found even more as we stepped inside the building. I safely tucked our soldier into my pocket, and we began picking up as many of the soldiers as we could, standing them upright around the giant leafy room. We stood them on every available surface, on rocks and on planks of fallen wood. We found some overturned tables, righted them, and covered them with more soldiers. The tiny armies grew and grew as we stood them in row after row. Everywhere we looked we found more tin soldiers, some holding guns, some holding flags, some astride tin horses, some kneeling and firing tin cannons. They all were scratched and faded and broken in one way or another. It was an army of tattered soldiers, like a huge family that had banded together and somehow survived the worst. We stood them on the windowsills and on the exposed beams in the walls. We grouped them by uniform, the blue ones over here, the red ones, like my soldier, over there. Some wore green, others gray, and they all had differently shaped hats and guns and flags. The neat rows of soldiers looked beautiful against the crazy zigzag of the branches and leaves.

"These are the Wild Prince's people," Ezra whispered. "They are all here. The Wild Prince isn't alone at all!"

I took the soldier out of my pocket and gently placed him down among his brothers.

Our soldier had found his home.

*　*　*

Ezra and I looked around us, and the sight was so beautiful, so dazzling, that we didn't see the thunderclouds gathering and we didn't notice that the light had changed. The green went out of the air and everything became gray. We nearly jumped out of our skins when the thunder finally roared, moments after the shocking white explosion of distant lightning. We screamed and grabbed onto each other. It was like an ocean had been safely tucked above us, and now someone had rudely ripped the bottom, sending all the water pouring down to earth. It got so dark and we were scared. We looked down for our soldier, but he was lost amid the others, and in the rain we couldn't find him anyway. I knew we were both thinking the same thing: *We can't leave him behind, and we can't stay here any longer.* We knew we'd come back, so we ran out of the forest, helping each other up when we fell.

Ezra and I ran to my house, where my mother was worried out of her mind. Ezra quickly called his own mother to say he was okay. My mom said he could sleep over, and his mom agreed. We took off our clothes so my mother could put them in the dryer, and I loaned him an outfit of mine to wear in the meantime. We ran to the window and watched the rain and the lightning.

Then our electricity went out.

My parents lit candles around the house, and in an odd way, it was nice. We had dinner by candlelight, but mostly we just watched the rain.

*   *   *

Suddenly lightning hit the forest. It was so bright and so loud that the house shook. We ran to the window and saw the most shocking thing we'd ever seen. The forest was on fire, right in the middle of the rainstorm. I didn't even know that was possible. The flames leaped up into the dark sky, angry orange columns that were beautiful and terrifying at the same time. We screamed and tried to run outside but were stopped by my parents, who thought we were crazy. The phones were out, so my mom had to find her cell phone to call the fire department.

Soon the firefighters came, driving their trucks as far as they could into the forest. It took a long time for the flames to die down. Ezra and I were out of our minds with worry. What had happened to our soldier? To the abandoned building?

* * *

When Ezra and I woke up the next morning, the rain had stopped and the sun was shining. We jumped up, got dressed, and ran outside, but there was yellow police tape at the edge of the forest. We snuck underneath it and ran through the forest to our building.

Our building was gone. It had burned to the ground, and between the fires and the floods, the soldiers were gone, too. We didn't know if they had melted away or were swept elsewhere by the water, but we overturned the few charred remains and found nothing. A police officer found us there and chased us out of the forest. We went home, sad and soldierless.

* * *

Eventually, Ezra's mom came and picked him up, and there was nothing to do at all.

But the next day the newspaper arrived with a thunk on the porch. My father got it, took it to the table as he always did, and opened it. "Well, how about that," he said. My mom and I went over to look. On the front page of the newspaper was a photograph of the fire from two nights earlier. The headline read: *Lightning Strikes Twice for Old Toy Company.*

We read the article.

Lightning does indeed strike twice, it began. *The night before last, lightning struck an abandoned toy factory here in town, exactly one hundred years to the day after first being struck. On June 3, 1904, lightning struck the Welcome Product Toy Company in the middle of the night. The fire raged for two days and brought children to the area for days afterward, scouring the ruins for abandoned toys . . .*

"Welcome Product . . . ," I said out loud. "WP."

* * *

The phone rang. Ezra had just read the article, too, but he said that wasn't what had really happened. At first I didn't understand what he was talking about, but then, as if he was reading from the newspaper, he told me what he said was the *true* story.

"The night before last," Ezra said, "the Wild Prince was at last reunited with his lost brothers. They were all so happy to finally be together again that they spent the night building a ship out of pieces of the abandoned toy factory where most of them had been hiding. But it wasn't a regular ship. It didn't float on water. This ship sailed on fire. When lightning struck the forest, they were able to sail away, all together. No one knows where they are going or how long it will take them to get there. The only thing we know is they are together and they are happy."

*   *   *

Even now, all these years later, I remember what Ezra said so perfectly, because it turns out that he was absolutely right.

FLIT
by Patrick Jennings

MONROE'S NEW SCHOOL, Tecumseh Junior High, was the same as the others: desk/chair hybrids, big clocks, a "bell" that went *boop*, banks of computers, tired teachers, dark halls, metal lockers, bulletin boards no one ever looked at, paper banners with positive messages (*"CAN I? I CAN!"*), an office with secretaries and a principal, a loud cafeteria serving beige food and half pints of milk, and bored and restless boys and girls. Already the new faces were blending with the old, each kid reminding Monroe of someone else he couldn't quite put his finger on. By lunch he had sorted out much of the cast: the Clowns, Pets, Bullies, Geeks, Freaks, Jocks, Brainiacs, etc. Monroe was the New Kid, and, unless he did something really stupid right off the bat, he could coast a day or two on the built-in mystique of being alien. Soon enough, though, he'd be labeled, like a can of soup. Which label depended a lot on who approached him first and how he responded, on whether or not he glad-handed the cool kids and shunned the uncool ones.

Monroe did not wish to make any enemies; neither did he wish to make any friends. He knew better than that, and if he ever forgot, Flit reminded him.

"Your mom didn't even bother to finish unpacking this time," Flit said.

It was true. Monroe's mom used the unopened boxes for shelves and end tables. This was the family's sixth move in four years.

One of the million Dylans that swarmed the country's middle schools approached Monroe at lunch. Monroe was sitting on a concrete bench, pretending to read a book — a sure way, he knew, to attract Geeks, Brainiacs, and, worst of all, girls, but also an escape from the attention of the dreaded Jocks and Bullies.

"What're you readin'?" the Dylan asked.

He looked much like dozens of other boys Monroe had known (in the broadest possible sense of the word). His hair was short, spiky, and dirt colored; freckles (and his breakfast) speckled his face; he lacked a tooth, a chin, and manners; he donned standard middle-school garb, including the same pricey aerodynamic sneakers worn by everyone their age (including Monroe), a black baseball cap (worn backward, of course), baggy jeans, and a baggy black T-shirt with a popular slogan (currently,

"*WHAT REGRETS?*") printed in red capitals on the front and a giant red question mark on the back.

"Loser," Flit whispered in Monroe's ear. "Shake him."

"A book," Monroe replied without looking up.

"I *thought* that's what that was," the Dylan said.

Signs of intelligence, Monroe thought. *Must be a Geek.* He kept his nose in the book.

The Dylan tilted his head, read the spine.

"You into fantasy?" he said. "Me, too. I'm going to be either a fantasy or horror writer. Can't decide which yet. Maybe I'll mix the two genres. I've already written seventy-four stories. Do you like dinosaurs?"

Geek, all right. Monroe turned the page — though he hadn't read a word on it — and feigned engrossment.

The Dylan proceeded to go into exhaustive detail about several of the stories he'd written, all of which featured dinosaurs, some of them mutant, others alien, or bioengineered, or "dinoid" (part dinosaur, part machine). The stories were distinguished by finely wrought gore and violence. The mad scrambling of headless victims figured prominently. Monroe made a good show of pretending that the Dylan was talking to someone else, though, in truth, he was listening intently, and with only mild revulsion. He wasn't immune to monstrous fantasies.

"Maybe he's hearing impaired," the Dylan said with a sigh of fake concern.

Monroe looked up, quickly realized his mistake, resubmerged.

"Nope," the Dylan said smugly. "Hearing intact."

He turned on his heel, walked away. Monroe peered over the top of his book, watching him go. Another, smaller red question mark was embroidered on the back — which is to say the front — of the kid's cap.

"I thought he'd never leave," Flit said. "What a geekazoid."

Monroe felt a twinge in his stomach. The Dylan hadn't seemed so bad, but you could never tell, and ditching a Geek was a lot harder than losing the bad rep you got from having befriended one. Monroe told himself he'd done the right thing.

No one else spoke to him the rest of the day. After the last *boop,* as he walked toward his latest apartment (not "home"), he tried to differentiate this new town from the last. The houses in both were rectangular, with rectangular windows and doors, the sidewalks gray and cracked, the streets black and wide. The grayish and bluish cars were shaped like last year's sneakers, as they had been in the last town. The stop signs were precisely the same.

Monroe let himself in with his key. His parents, of course, were not home. His dad was a salesman for a beauty supply company out of Lansing, where the family had once lived, and worked "long hours." (*Aren't they all long?* Monroe mused.) His dad was clearly a bad salesman. Why else would he get transferred so often? Monroe's mom, like Monroe himself, was a temp.

He dropped his backpack on the floor of his room, sank onto the bed, and stared at the ghosts of picture frames on the blank white plaster wall. The first day of school was always the longest. At the end of each he always told himself he'd never, ever go back again. But he always did.

"That wasn't very much fun, now was it?" Flit said, materializing on Monroe's knee in his customary puff of green smoke. "You were right to brush off that Dylan. As a rule, the first ones to introduce themselves are the worst. Obviously, he's friendless, probably for very good reasons. Why else would he pounce on fresh meat like us?"

Flit could always be counted on to look on the bleak side. Not that Monroe really believed anymore that Flit had his own opinions. He knew that when he listened or talked to Flit he was conversing with himself. Despite this, he had come to see Flit as a distinct person with a distinct personality, a person whose remarks at times genuinely surprised him.

Flit had been Monroe's imaginary pixie friend since before Monroe could remember. When he was little, Flit was as real as anyone, as real as rain. But then, at around the time that Monroe's fervent beliefs in Santa Claus, the Sandman, and the Tooth Fairy were dashed on the rocks of disappointment and betrayal, Flit burst Monroe's remaining bubble.

"Don't you get it yet?" Flit said to him. "I'm not real, chum. I'm a figment of your imagination."

But Monroe kept alive the little guy with the green leotard, the shimmery green dragonfly wings, and the tiny green almond-shaped eyes. He had to; he was friendless.

Monroe had frightful nightmares — and day-mares — in which classmates overheard him talking to Flit. The chorus of ridicule would then shake him awake. Being found to have an imaginary friend was Monroe's worst fear.

Once, however, he did tell someone. He still couldn't guess what had possessed him to do such a stupid thing. Just the thought of it made him wince.

The girl's name was Candelaria. She attended the school before last, in the town before last, though she hadn't attended it long. Her family had moved there from Guatemala only months before Monroe's family had arrived. She was skittish as a squirrel, never spoke to anyone. Against Flit's advice, and despite her being a girl, Monroe befriended her. She barely spoke English, so, for a quarter, Monroe purchased a small dog-eared paperback Spanish-English dictionary at a thrift store. They passed the dictionary back and forth as they talked. She said he could call her Candy. She pronounced his name "Moanrow." Not speaking the same language proved to be a blessing in disguise. Conversation between them required real patience, concentration, and commitment. Due to this, they never wasted words. They cut straight to the things that mattered: where they were, how they felt about being there, what they had left behind.

Candy was hard on herself when she spoke incorrect English.

"The food is no the same here," Candelaria said once.

"*Not* the same," Monroe corrected.

"Excuse me, please. The food is *not* the same," she said, echoing his intonation.

"*Bueno,*" Monroe said.

"Only speak in English, please. I need to learn."

"Sorry. Good."

Candy looked up, her eyes closed. "I want the sun," she said.

"We have the sun here," Monroe said.

She shook her head. "No the same sun."

"*Not.*"

She blushed, opened her big, inky eyes. "Excuse me, please. *Not* the same sun."

Monroe decided her determination to speak properly meant she was proud. He liked that. Most kids were cocky, not proud. She acted older than anyone in their class, more poised, calmer. She had great posture. Monroe liked that, too.

One day, after she had told him about her rag doll, Lalo, that she still slept with and sang to, he found himself telling her about Flit. Candy promised to keep Flit a secret till she was *muerto,* dead. Monroe felt relieved after telling her — for a couple of seconds. Then panic set in. Flit sure gave him an earful about it.

"That was the single dumbest thing you've ever done in your whole stupid life," he said. "She blabs and our lives are ruined."

Monroe was terrified. He decided to keep his mouth shut about Flit forevermore. Meanwhile, his bad dreams intensified.

A week later, his mom told him that they were moving again. Monroe blew a sigh of relief. Flit firmly believed that Monroe should not tell Candy they were leaving.

"What's to keep her from telling the secret then? She'll spread it all over school before you can say, 'Freaky kid talks to pixies.'"

"What difference would it make?" Monroe argued. "We're leaving anyway. And besides, Candy would never do something like that."

"'Trust no one,'" Flit said. "That's rule number one. Rule number two is also 'Trust no one.' We move in a week. Keep your big trap shut about it."

In order to do that, Monroe had to avoid Candy completely. It was the nature of their friendship to be candid, to talk about personal, private, important things Monroe never told anyone (though Flit eavesdropped on every moment of his life). Monroe left town without speaking another word to Candy, without saying good-bye. This hurt more than he could have thought possible.

"There," Flit said smugly. "Now aren't you glad you made a friend?"

Jigsaw puzzles helped relieved the ache, if only temporarily. Monroe had done them for years. Assembling a puzzle left little room in his mind for anything else. His latest had a thousand pieces, each identical in shape and size. His only guide was a picture on the box of a lime-green chameleon on a lime-green leaf.

The second day at Tecumseh Junior High felt shorter by half. *Anything can be made routine,* Monroe thought. *Even change.*

He kept to his book, kept to himself. The Dylan had gotten the message and stayed away, as did pretty much everyone else. Two girls approached Monroe once. Like him, they wore glasses. He sympathized. They wanted to know what he was reading.

"Tell 'em to take a hike," Flit hissed into his ear.

"Take a hike," Monroe said to them.

He'd learned his lesson. Henceforth he'd listen to Flit.

The verdict arrived the following Monday, during lunch, when Monroe overheard someone say "Bookworm" as he passed a group of sniggering boys in the hall. He heard the word again later from a giggling gaggle of girls. (Taylor, Reagan, and Madison. Naming girls after presidents had apparently been the thing to do the year Monroe was born. Was it inevitable he'd one day meet a girl called Eisenhower? Or Monroe?) The label had been printed, peeled, and affixed: In this school, in this town, Monroe was a Bookworm.

He didn't mind. Being a Bookworm was easy and relatively safe. When he'd been a Brainiac, kids pestered him for help with their homework or for answers on their tests. When he was a Geek, his books were kicked out of his hands, his chair jerked out from under him, his back used as a bulletin board for sticky notes reading, for example, *"SNORT IF YOU LIKE GEEKS"* or *"TRIP ME."* Bookworms, in general, received fewer peer humiliations. All that would be required of him as a Bookworm was to sit off by himself and burrow into books. He took to checking out the biggest, fattest ones in the library. Fantasy series were best. They gave the impression that reading was not only his life but also his career path. He didn't read the books, of course; he just flipped their pages.

Three weeks passed. The only friend he made was the librarian, and that was only because she was deluded into thinking he was a voracious reader. No one talked to him. Only occasionally did some Jock or Bully send his big books flying down the halls.

And then one day in language arts, during Free Reading Time (which everyone smirkingly pronounced as an acronym), the Dylan walked up to Monroe's desk/chair and pointed at the book he wasn't reading.

"*Dude,* that is like my *all-time* favorite series in the history of the world," he said. "Maybe when you're done we could, like, discuss it."

"Uh, sure," escaped Monroe's lips. Talking was strictly verboten during FRT, but the kid had caught him by surprise.

"Dylan?" the teacher said. "Don't you have anything to read this morning?"

The class hissed and hooted. Monroe's face burned with embarrassment.

"The bookshelf is full to bursting," the teacher said.

"Naw," the Dylan said. "I got something." He hung his head and shuffled back to his desk.

It was a few minutes before Monroe's nerves had calmed enough for him to refocus on the opened slab of words in front of him. *Maybe I'll actually read some of them,* he thought.

The book was the first of a tetralogy, called *The Cleiedo Quartet.* Monroe had no idea how to pronounce

Cleiedo ("Clee-*eye*-doh"? "Cly-*ee*-doh"? "*Clee*-aid-o"? "*Cly*-doh"?). Each volume was well over four hundred pages long; the last was well over six. Each contained detailed maps, diagrams, and genealogies. Many of the characters' names appeared to be anagrams of normal names: Knive, Baltar, Irch, Vadide, Teka. The story took place on a planet (Cleiedo) that was a lot like Earth except there were dragons, mages, androids, a miniature race of gnomelike creatures, and a couple of extra moons. Monroe was surprised to discover there were no dinosaurs, though the dragons were kind of like fire-breathing pteranodons. There were several quests going on at once and just about everyone was trying to fulfill his or her own destiny. Making sense of it all proved more distracting than jigsaw puzzles. It wasn't long before Monroe was genuinely engrossed.

"I know what you're trying to do," Flit said. "You're trying to give you and that Dylan something in common. Bad idea, friend. What happens when you guys are bosom buddies and suddenly Dad gets another transfer?"

Monroe tried not to think about that as he finished Volume One, *The Dragons of Cleiedo*, and dived into Volume Two, *The Oracle of Cleiedo*. A week later he'd finished the third book, *The Siege of Cleiedo*, and was deep into the fourth and final installment, *The Fate of Cleiedo.* He was spending every unoccupied moment on a strange, faraway planet: while eating breakfast, on the way to school, in the cafeteria, in FRT, on the way home. It was the happiest he'd been since Candy.

At first, Flit was merely irritated by Monroe's new "waste of time." When Monroe kept on with it, though, Flit took first to lecturing him, then to scolding him, then to whining, "Why are you ignoring me? Don't forget, I'm the only real friend you've got!"

"Not now, Flit," Monroe told him, waving him off.

Flit brooded and sulked. Sometimes he poofed off, not returning for long stretches at a time.

Monroe took advantage of the quiet. Despite his best efforts to pace himself, he sped toward the finish of the last book. He wanted to know how it ended; he didn't want it to end.

The Dylan hadn't spoken to Monroe since that day in FRT, but Monroe caught him eyeing his bookmark, watching it as it inched toward the back. Monroe was bursting to talk to him about it. He had so many burning questions: Would Knive rescue Teka? Could Teka be trusted? Was Orquidea (a dragon) tamable? Could Knive foil the evil mage Irch and his army of man/mongoose half breeds, thereby ending Irch's tyranny over

Cleiedo while also fulfilling Knive's own destiny? Monroe didn't ask, though. He wanted to find out for himself. Afterward he and the Dylan could discuss the series unguardedly and at length.

Monroe came to the last chapter on a Wednesday, at midnight, hunched under his covers with his key ring flashlight. He shut the book without the bookmark — he knew where he'd left off — turned off the light, whispered to himself, "*Tomorrow*," then fell asleep, cuddling the fat book as if it were a teddy bear.

When, disappointingly, the Dylan wasn't at school the next day, Monroe forced himself to read no more than a paragraph of the remaining chapter per hour, even if the paragraph was a single line of dialogue. He forsook this rationing when school let out. The yawning afternoon was too distractionless. He reached the final page leaning out his bedroom window, straining to read the words under the last rays of the sun. (He couldn't be bothered to stop and switch on a lamp.) The climax had been everything he'd hoped it would be: shocking, horrifying, bloody, triumphant. Irch had been destroyed so that not a particle of him remained anywhere in the universe. Knive had not married Teka, as Monroe feared he might, for the simple reason that she turned out to be — a machine! Of *course!* Orquidea the dragon proved to be the most trustworthy friend a man could ever have.

Monroe sprawled out on his back on the bed, drained and exhilarated, replaying snatches of the story on the stuccoed ceiling. He hoped upon hope that the Dylan would return to class the next day, that he didn't have the flu or some fatal disease.

He didn't. It was far worse than that. The homeroom teacher announced the next morning that Dylan Workman and his family had moved away.

"No," Monroe said aloud.

Everyone turned and looked at him. Some snickered. Monroe didn't care. What did it matter? Dylan — *the* Dylan — was gone. Monroe had read the books for nothing.

"I hope you learned a valuable lesson here," Flit whispered in his ear.

He had.

He returned the final volume to the library.

"What did you think?" the librarian asked eagerly.

Monroe said nothing. He walked away, gathered up a new series — a pentalogy — and dumped the doorstops on the checkout counter.

"You'll like this one," the librarian said less enthusiastically as she wanded the books.

"I doubt it," Monroe said. "I have no intention of reading it."

Over the next month Monroe assembled four thousand-piece puzzles, including one that had no picture. It was a two-foot-by-three-foot rectangle of cardboard painted solid red. He was biding his time till his dad's next transfer.

Monroe's mom came into his room one Saturday morning as he was turning the two thousand pieces of his new puzzle picture-side-up. Monroe stared up at her, stunned. His mom never came into his room. She was wearing a blue blazer-and-skirt suit with blue pumps and black nylons. Her makeup and perfume were heavy, as was her expression. She couldn't know how desperately Monroe had been awaiting her "bad news."

"You got a letter, honey," she said, and set a white envelope atop his puzzle pieces. She kissed his brow and left.

Monroe sat there, blinking. Not only had he been expecting to hear something entirely different, but he also had never gotten a letter from anyone in his life — other than his grandparents, which didn't count.

The letter was from Candy. He ripped it open and unfolded the sheet of paper within to find a short, typewritten note. In trying to absorb all the words at once, he was unable to comprehend a single one. He shut his eyes, told himself to breathe, then tried again.

> Dear Monroe,
>
> I got you address for our teacher. I hope you don't care. I was sad you left not saying good-bye. I guess you were to sad. I think much about you. You are my best amigo in America. (Excuse the Spanish please.)
>
> Write back soon,
> Sincerely,
> Candi
>
> P.S. — Lalo says Hi. Say Hi to Flit for me, too.

Candi, Monroe thought. *With an* i, *not a* y.

He read the letter over six more times, then set it down, brushed the puzzle pieces aside, got out paper and a pen, and wrote a long reply.

Flit appeared on the paper in a green puff. "What are you doing? Don't you ever learn?"

"Not now, Flit," Monroe said, nudging him away with his pen.

After reading back the letter he'd written, he spiced it up with words from his dog-eared Spanish-English dictionary. Then he began another letter, this one to Dylan. He went into great detail about what he thought of the *The Cleiedo Quartet.* Then he ran to the desk in the den for envelopes. He copied Candi's address onto one. He'd get Dylan's at school on Monday.

As Monroe was folding Candi's letter, Flit rematerialized. He didn't look scornful. His hands were folded in front of him.

"Can you tell her 'Hi' back?" he said, looking at his feet.

Monroe nodded, and added a P.S. He put the letters into the envelopes, sealed them, and affixed two self-adhesive postage stamps.

He fell onto his bed, opened to the first page of the first book of the new pentalogy he'd been pretending to read. Flit appeared on his shoulder. They read in silence.

THE JUSTICE LEAGUE
by David Levithan

I WAS THE LOUD ONE. Tim was the smart one and I was the loud one. Tim was the thin one and I was the loud one. Tim was the quiet, shy, careful one. And I was the one who could never sit still. Not just my body. My mind couldn't sit still.

But wherever I was, Tim was there beside me. Ever since we were little kids in preschool. Tim arranged blocks into tidy skyscrapers. I threw blocks around. In first grade, second grade, third grade — he liked to sit in a corner during recess, drawing kingdoms and monsters. I played on every team possible. Everywhere at once. Yelling for the ball.

After school we would go over to his house and play video games and watch TV and, when his mom was around, do our homework. When his mom was out of the room I copied down what he wrote. He didn't mind. But he always made sure to tell me how I could get the right answers. He said that was the point. I thought the point was getting it done.

Fourth grade. Tim and I were in the same class, like always. It was as if the principal and all the teachers knew we couldn't be separated. It's not that we didn't have other friends — I, at least, had a lot of other friends. A whole team's worth. And Tim — well, Tim had books. And he had girls like Carla Gilman and Alison Gould, who also had books. They were never reading the same thing at the same time, but the way they sat together on the outer edge of the football field, you would've thought they were.

Tim was my secret language friend. Guys like Rob and Devon were my first-draft-pick friends. And guys like Wes and Braden were the ones who were never quite friends but were always on my team. They thought I was fine, and they thought Tim was less than a worm.

The trouble started late in fourth grade. One lunchtime, Ms. Cross kept me a few minutes late because I'd been shouting answers without raising my hand first. I had no way to explain to her the reason I'd shouted out was because I'd been so surprised and happy that I'd actually *known* who was president in 1900 and who was president in 1950. By the time I got to the lunchroom, there weren't any turkey sandwiches left, and Wes was pouring chocolate milk down Tim's shirt. Carla and

Alison were looking on with horror, and Braden was looking on with a big grin on his face. I skipped the lunch line and headed over to our usual table. Wes stopped pouring when he saw me, but he didn't hide the carton or anything.

"What's going on?" I asked.

I tried to read Tim's expression, but our secret language was failing. It was like trying to watch a TV show on a TV set that isn't on.

"Nothing," Wes said. "Just giving Tim some chocolate milk."

He said this like it made total sense.

"Down his back?" I asked.

"Yeah." Braden giggled. "*Down his back.*"

Then both he and Wes started guffawing. Like I'd just given them the punch line to the joke.

But that wasn't the kind of punch I felt like giving.

I knocked the chocolate milk carton out of Wes's hand, so it spilled on his leg on the way to the floor.

"Not funny," I said.

"Dude!" he said. "It was only a joke."

"Not funny," I repeated, standing my ground.

Wes shrugged. Then he leaned over, patted Tim on the head, and said, "See you later, loser."

I continued standing there until they left.

"Are you okay?" I asked Tim.

I expected him to be happy with me for chasing them away. Or at least relieved. But instead he looked at me blankly. No *thank you*. No joke. Just quiet. Absolute quiet.

I figured he didn't want to talk about it. I went to get my lunch and brought him back napkins to wipe things up with. He took them, but then started talking about the latest *Justice League of America.* I steered the conversation to *X-Men,* and then when recess came he went off with Carla and Alison, while I hit the field with Rob and Devon and Wes and Braden.

Nothing else was said. Not until after school, when Tim and I were walking to his house. His shirt still had a brown streak on it from where the chocolate milk had settled in. I knew he couldn't see it, but I was sure he knew it was there.

"Don't do that again," he said as we hit his street.

"What?" I asked.

"I can handle them," he told me. And because he was my best friend, I didn't say, *No, you can't.*

For the rest of fourth grade, Wes and Braden picked on Tim, but only in the same way that they picked on everyone else. Predictably, Tim and I reacted differently to this. When Wes or Braden knocked my books off my desk, I made sure to knock their books back — as if taunting was like playing on a seesaw. When Tim's books were knocked over, he would just pick them up and rearrange them as if nothing had happened. When he looked at Wes and Braden, it was like he couldn't even remember their names.

We never talked about this. We had our superheroes instead — their secret identities, their last-ditch efforts to save the world, the times they turned evil, and the strength that brought them back to good.

When we hit fifth grade, we became the oldest kids in the school. I loved that. I did safety patrol in the morning, because I liked the idea that I could stop traffic (even though we were told to never, ever do this). At recess, I felt like I owned the field. In class, I couldn't sit still. Our teacher, Mr. Carlsbad, was always telling me to hush, to wait my turn. But I never knew when my turn was supposed to be. I only knew what *now* meant.

Rob brought a handball in one day, and soon all of us were playing handball nonstop at recess. There was one spot in the back of the school where a perfect square of wall met a perfect square of blacktop. With the recess supervisor's permission, we brought some chalk outside and made a handball court. I tried to get Tim to play, but he had just inherited all of his brother's old comic books, so he was bringing them to school ten at a time to read. I think he wanted me to read them with him, but in the end he understood my absence in the same way that I understood him not going near the handball court; he had his thing and I had mine. After school, we hung out like we always had. But in school, we became more separate.

Wes and Braden were not big fans of handball, because it stole people away from football and because — it only took one game to notice — they weren't nearly as good at it. Rob, who caught one out of four football passes on a good day, was suddenly our recess champion. I was a close second. Something about handball was perfect for me — rushing from corner to corner, whacking the ball with my palm, then running to anticipate the next shot. There was no time to think, only time to move. That worked for me.

After a week of this, Wes and Braden drifted off. First they returned to the field, passing the football back and forth to each other until that got boring. Then they drifted to the girls playing jump rope, making fun of their rhymes with some nasty verses of their own. Then they made their way to Carly and Alison and called them losers. And finally they got to Tim.

I didn't notice at first. I didn't notice until Rob noticed and pointed in Tim's direction. Wes and Braden had grabbed two of Tim's comic books and were dangling them over Tim's head.

"Give them back," he said.

"Why should we?" Wes teased.

"Because they belong to me," Tim replied. As if that would be that.

"Fine," Wes said. And then he gave the comic back . . . one page at a time. That first rip was like a gunshot to me. I was totally surprised by it, and so was Tim. Even Wes seemed a little surprised. But that surprise egged him on. He wanted more of it. So he ripped and crumpled and ripped again.

Tim was standing now. With one swift move, he reached out and grabbed the comic back from Wes. Then he turned and grabbed the other one from Braden before he, too, could start ripping

Tim was about to sit back down when Wes shoved him to the ground.

Suddenly my mind jumped to action. I was about to yell. I was about to run over and shove Wes back.

Then I remembered what Tim had said. *I can handle them.* Did that still count in fifth grade?

"You think you're cool, huh?" Wes shouted. He knew we were all watching now. He knew we'd seen Tim take the comic back.

Tim chose to ignore him. He gathered all his comics up and opened the top one to read.

"That's it!" Wes was really angry now. "You and me. *After school.*"

He didn't need to say anything else. We all knew what this meant: Tim would have to meet him ten minutes after the last bell rang, in the wooded spot behind the baseball field that was hidden from the school windows. They'd fight things out with a crowd watching. This was how fifth graders handled things.

Tim knew, too.

And still he said no.

He said it so softly that nobody else could hear. I only knew what he said because I knew how to read him, even from far away.

"What did you say?" Wes shot out.

"I said 'no,'" Tim replied, louder now and clear. "I'm not going to fight you."

"Well, you're going to have to," Wes insisted.

"Why?" Tim asked.

"Because I SAID SO." Wes took a deep breath. "And if you don't show up . . . well, you better."

He pulled back his leg a little, as if he was getting ready to kick Tim. I bolted forward, but the kick was just a fake-out. Tim flinched and Wes laughed. Then Wes and Braden headed back to the field.

I waited a minute, until they were gone and people had stopped watching. I didn't want it to look like I was running to help Tim. Carly and Alison didn't hesitate — even before Wes and Braden were ten steps away, they had swooped in to collect some of the pages that had fallen and blown away. I picked the last one off the ground and handed it back to Tim.

"Thanks," he said.

"No problem."

"You know I'm not going to be there," he told me right away.

"You have to," I said. Everyone knew this: If you were challenged to a fight, you had to go.

"Actually," he said, "I don't have to."

"I can help," I offered.

I'd witnessed one of the behind-the-baseball-field fights before. It was when we were in third grade. There was a stretch where Tim had to go to piano lessons straight from school, so I was on my own. I saw that other kids were leaving school and going straight to the woods. Since I didn't have any bus to catch or anyone waiting for me to get home, I decided to follow.

Everyone had crowded into a rough circle. I didn't know whether this was so everyone could see or to keep the two combatants stuck inside the center. Two fifth graders were facing off; I quickly learned that the argument had started between Chris Kelly and Frank Dukes when Chris fouled Frank during gym class. Then the argument broadened out to include Chris calling Frank names and Frank calling Chris's mother names, until the shout-out had occurred and Chris had laid down the challenge to a fight. Frank had eagerly accepted.

Now they were staring each other down and nobody knew what to do. It wasn't like there was a ref to get things going or a starting gun to be fired. Instead there were just two boys stuck in the middle of a crowd, calling each other names. Then Chris lunged forward and Frank dug in his feet. Some people yelled, "Go, Chris!" and some people yelled, "Go, Frank!" Others whooped and others stayed silent. Chris's arm wobbled as he threw his fist out. Frank teetered as he waited for it to land. I had expected something like a boxing fight from the movies. Quick jabs. Strategy. But this wasn't like that at all. Chris's fist grazed off Frank's face. Frank jumped on him. And before any of us knew it, they were down on the ground, pummeling and kicking and rolling and ripping at each other's shirts. None of us knew how it was supposed to end. A teacher spotted our crowd and came running over. We opened the rough circle and let her through. "Stop it!" she yelled, over and over. Another teacher ran over and split Chris and Frank up. There were dirt stains all over their bodies, and Chris had a little bit of blood coming out of his lip. The second teacher dragged them down to the office while the first teacher told us all to go home, right this instant. I figured Chris and Frank would be back the next day to finish it off, to fight until there was a winner. But as far as I knew, they never did.

Now it was Tim and Wes who were going to be in that circle, and it didn't take a genius to know what the outcome would be. Still, Tim had to show up. It was an unwritten rule.

"I can show you how to hit," I said. "I'll back you up."

"No," Tim told me again. "You don't need to do that. I won't be there."

People knew we were friends. Throughout the rest of the school day, kids came up to me to ask if Tim was going to be there. And I was stuck. Because I knew that if I said yes, I would be lying. And I knew if I said no, it would only make things worse. So I said I didn't know.

Wes came up to me and said I'd better make sure Tim was there. I should have been able to put him in his place. But instead I shrugged. I said it was up to Tim.

"You have to," I told him toward the end of the day, when he passed the spelling quiz back to me.

You can't back down, I wrote in a note that I passed when we were taking out our history books.

"You'll be there, right?" I whispered when there were ten minutes left in school.

And he didn't even turn around. He just shook his head.

No.

When the bell rang, Wes made sure to come up to Tim's desk and say, "See you in ten minutes. Or else."

Tim shook his head again.

We were soon the last two kids in the classroom. Everyone else left to get a good watching spot.

"I'm going home," Tim said, putting his books in his knapsack. "Are you coming?"

"Everyone will make fun of you," I argued. "They'll say you're scared. That you knew you were going to lose. So you ran away."

Tim looked at me with this sad look in his eyes. Not sad with himself, but sad with me.

"Don't you get it?" he said. "Fighting doesn't stop

anything. If I go there, it doesn't matter if I win or lose. He wins because he gets to boss me into fighting him. And that's wrong. That's not . . . justice."

Justice was one of our big comic book words. I didn't see what it had to do with meeting Wes behind the baseball field.

"If you beat Wes up, *that* will be justice," I said.

"No. It's like making a war just so you can win it. You shouldn't make the war in the first place."

"What are you *talking about*?" I yelled. But then I stopped. Because I took a long, hard look at my friend and saw that he was shaking. Not on the outside, but on the inside. I realized I could push him into doing it. I realized he would listen to me. He would give in.

But I also realized that it would be just that — *giving in.* To Wes. To Braden. And, worst of all, to me.

"Fine," I said. "Let's go home."

I knew what would happen. I knew people would see us leave. I knew people would see *me* leave. I wish I could say I didn't care. I cared. I cared to the point that I almost turned the other way. I was ready to run to the woods and say, *Tim can't make it, but I'll fight for him instead.*

But instead I followed Tim out the door and away from the school. Neither of us looked back.

We didn't talk much on the walk home. When we

got to his house, we had a snack and read some of his brother's old comic books. And suddenly it was like I was reading them a new way. Spider-Man never picked a fight just to win a fight. The Fantastic Four only put themselves on the line when there was something big at stake. They stuck together. The X-Men were freaks because they wouldn't play by the evil masterminds' rules. But that's also why they were heroes.

When I got home, there was a message from Rob, telling me to call him right away. I did, and he told me what had happened when Tim hadn't shown up. There were about thirty kids there. Wes had made himself look all tough, rolling up his shirtsleeves to show his biceps. ("What biceps?" I asked Rob. "I have no idea," he said.)

Five minutes passed. Ten minutes passed. Wes went ballistic. He called Tim all kinds of names. Everybody walked away.

"It was really stupid," Rob said.

"I bet everyone thinks Tim's a loser now," I said.

"Actually," Rob told me, "he looks like the smart one. It was just so . . . lame, you know?"

I was sure this would make Wes even angrier. And I guess Tim knew this, too, since he was careful not to show up to class the next morning until Mr. Carlsbad was there and paying attention. This didn't stop Wes and Braden from hissing threats whenever Mr. C. was distracted. But they couldn't actually get to Tim. Not until lunch.

Right before the lunch bell, Tim passed me a note. *Don't fight him for me,* it said.

Then another note.

Ok?

And I answered.

OK.

Lunch brought the verbal threats.

"You're dead," Wes pronounced.

"Yeah, dead," Braden echoed.

Carly and Alison looked more worried than Tim did. I imagine I looked mad.

At recess, Tim sat down in his usual spot. This time, however, he hadn't brought anything but his homework to read — he didn't want to put any of the comic books at risk. Rob, Devon, and I didn't even pretend to start our handball game. We stayed close, waiting to see what would happen.

It didn't take Wes and Braden long. As soon as the recess supervisor was off patrolling the second graders on the jungle gym, they headed straight for Tim.

"You think you can just get out of it?" Wes asked. "You think you can just avoid me? Well, think again."

It sounded like he'd practiced these words. A rehearsed tough guy.

"I'm not going to fight you," Tim murmured.

Wes laughed. "You think you have a choice?"

"I'm not going to fight just because you say we have to." Tim's voice grew louder now, so all of us could hear. "That's stupid."

"You think I'm stupid?" Wes shouted. He hovered over Tim and stepped on his textbook. "Do you?"

I thought, *I can take him.* Wes was about my size, but I had power on my side. A simple tackle. A shot to the eye. Bruise him. Hurt him. Teach him.

But then I saw Tim looking at me. And looking at Rob and Devon and Carly and everyone else who was watching. Everyone but Wes.

"ANSWER ME!" Wes screamed. And then he kicked Tim, right in the stomach.

And I knew. Tim didn't want me to lunge in, punch back. Fine.

That wouldn't stop me from being loud.

"YOU ARE SUCH A LOSER!" I yelled.

Wes stopped.

"What did you say?" he asked me, snarling out the question.

"You're kicking someone while he's *sitting down?*" I shouted. "How cool does that make you, Wes? How much strength does *that* take?"

Bruise him.

"We're sick of you, Wes," I broadcast across the school yard. "We're *all* sick of you."

Hurt him.

"Do *you* want to fight, Burgess?" Wes yelled back. "'Cause don't think I'm scared."

"I'm *not* going to fight you," I said. "Can't you see that's the point?"

"We're through with you," Rob chimed in.

"Yeah," Devon added.

Teach him.

I almost felt sorry for Wes. He didn't know what to do. And Braden was even more clueless, following his lead.

Tim stood up then. He was wincing a little — that kick had landed hard. But he stood up on his own and didn't even keep his eye on Wes or Braden. They were done.

Instead Tim took the few steps over to us. He looked at Rob and asked, "Can you teach me handball?"

And Rob said, "Sure."

I continued to stare Wes down. I continued to

watch as he just stood there. He yelled a few more things — insults, threats. But it was like the words had lost all their muscle. They were empty bodies, useless.

To get pulled into a fight you can't win — that doesn't make you a loser. Even if you lose.

To pull someone into a fight just to prove you're stronger — well, that *does* make you a loser. Even if you win.

I don't think Tim meant to make me realize this. I think he only wanted to explain why he wasn't going to fight Wes in the woods after school that day. But maybe that's a part of the secret language of friendship — there are lessons in what you choose to do and what you choose not to do. You don't need a cape to be a crusader. You don't need a nemesis in order to do what's right.

And the lessons aren't one way, either. Tim never really learned how to be good at handball. But in time, he did learn this:

When justice is at stake, there are times when you need to be loud.

MINKA AND MEANIE
by Rachel Cohn

ONLY A LAP CURL FROM MEANIE THE CAT and a swear-to-God cross-my-heart promise from Andrew that he would take her to the Polish church in Greenpoint on Sunday got Minka to agree to baby-sit me today.

Minka doesn't like children. She came all the way to America from Poland to be with her grandchildren in Chicago. She only survived a month in Chicago before showing up at our apartment in Brooklyn. According to Minka (by way of Andrew's translation), her Chicago grandchildren ran wild in the house and acted embarrassed when their friends came over and Minka only spoke Polish. Proper grandchildren should be respectful of their elders, she said, and should know how to say "please" and "thank you," preferably in Polish. They should go to religious school every Sunday instead of to soccer games, and they should never pass over their grandmother's homemade babka in favor of Oreos.

Minka doesn't like cats, either, which is fine by Meanie, because he doesn't like people unless they're delivering his Fancy Feast. Only then will he bother to look a person in the eyes, as if to say, *Well, I suppose I can let you do me this favor.* For a person who hates cats and a cat who hates persons, Minka and Meanie have become pretty much inseparable since Minka arrived at our apartment.

At first Andrew said we might have to get rid of Meanie when Minka came to stay, because of her cat issues. So I threw what Mom calls one of my "epic screaming fits," and Meanie was safe for the time being. I think Minka would have taken over my room if she could have, but I sleep on a loft bed in a room that's barely the size of a closet and Minka has a fear of heights and enclosed spaces.

When she arrived, Minka didn't know Meanie already had permanent dibs on the certain spot on the couch where he liked to snooze at night. Minka just took that spot over, TV remote clicker in hand, as if it belonged to her, without so much as asking his permission. Meanie used to hiss at Minka, and she sneezed and coughed all night long on the couch pullout bed from Meanie's cat hair. Then Mom gave Minka a prescription for allergies and I guess Meanie decided if you can't beat 'em, join 'em. Now the two of them curl next to each other on the couch instead of snarling at each other. I think she feeds him treats when we're not looking. He was a fat cat before she came, but now he's huge, like a beast.

Minka complains all the time, but since I don't speak Polish the complaining doesn't annoy me as much as it bothers Andrew. Maybe that's because Andrew's her son who's been hearing it for a lifetime, and I'm only the daughter of her son's girlfriend who doesn't understand her anyway.

I expected the snow that fell today, piles and piles of white glory, would cause Minka to do her usual grumble of, "*Dlaczego? Dlaczego? Dlaczego?*" ("*Why? Why? Why?*" according to Andrew.) Instead, I went into the kitchen and saw Minka waving to me through the glass door from the patio outside. She sat on the patio chair wearing her robe and slippers, smoking, her white-blond hair specked with thick snowflakes, her rosy cheeks flaming red. When I opened the door, she didn't whine, "*Dlaczego?*" She gestured to the snow and said in her deep, smoky voice, "Bee-yew-tee-ful, yez?"

I said, "Minka, it's cold outside; you should be wearing a coat and proper boots!"

She rapid-mumbled something in Polish, something I was fairly sure translated as, "You only nine years old; what you know? It your mother fault I freeze out here, just because she doctor, so high-and-mighty, with her no-smoking-in-house rule. When my son Andrzej was doctor in Poland, before he come to this country and must start all over again, Andrzej not care if I smoke in house."

The radio announced no school today, but that didn't mean the hospital closed. Andrew and Mom both had to work, and it took a ten-minute powwow with them, Minka, and Meanie to get Minka to agree (without consulting me, of course) to stay home with me. I wanted to say, "*Of course* Minka would agree to 'baby-sit' — where else does she have to go!?" You could take Minka to the best places, to the Mermaid Parade at Coney Island or to Madame Tussaud's in Times Square or to Game 7 of a Mets–Yankees subway classic, and she would still have that sour look on her face. She gives these *looks* that speak louder than her few English words ("NO!" "YEZ!" "REGIS!"), looks that tell you she'd rather be sitting in some grimy, gray Warsaw café eating cabbage, smoking, and gossiping in Polish than witnessing the great new world right in front of her.

I thought, *It's Minka who needs the baby-sitter, not me.* I had places to go on a snow day, not that anyone asked my opinion. I wouldn't have minded taking the train into Manhattan to make snowmen in Central Park, followed by a giant ice-cream sundae at Serendipity. Who cared how cold it was outside? I could have gone to Chrissy's to play, even though I never know if she'll be nice Chrissy or mean Chrissy when I show up at her house or if she's going to share her Barbies with me or poke me in the eye with their slippers. Or I could just sneak into a movie I wasn't old enough to see and stay at the movies all day, safe and happy, with no baby-sitter!

But no, I got stuck with Minka and Meanie. I was pouting on my bed after Mom and Andrew left for work when I looked down to see Minka standing at the doorway. She refuses to step all the way inside my tiny room, which is only big enough to fit a loft bed, a desk under the bed, some dresser drawers against the wall, and a person standing sideways.

"Katya," she said, even though she knows my name is Kate, "lezgo." I just looked at her like, WHAT? Minka walked down the hall and I heard her open the hall closet. She returned to the doorway holding my snowsuit. I jumped off that loft bed so fast that Meanie himself, purring by Minka's side, jumped a little, too — just not a big jump on account of how big he's gotten.

Mom and Andrew think all Minka does during the

day while I'm at school and they're at work is sleep, smoke, and watch TV. They enrolled her in an English class nearby, but the school called to say she never showed. Now I know why. Minka spends her days with Meanie at the coffee shop on the corner. No, really.

I had dressed in my snowsuit and was waiting for Minka to join me outside when she came out of our brownstone dressed in a parka and trailing Meanie, who was attached to . . . a LEASH! A CAT! And not just any cat, but Meanie, who hisses if you try to remove him from the sunny windowsill. He likes to perch there during the day to stare down birds and squirrels and normally would not budge from that spot if the house were on fire. But no, he was outside, trailing alongside Minka — and in the snow, no less! This was obviously not the first time Minka and Meanie were taking a neighborhood stroll together.

One awesome quality about Minka is that I can say anything to her. I could say, "Minka, are you aware that you're making Mom crazy? You've been with us a month and have yet to say whether your visit is permanent or temporary. Mom's trying to be cool about you being at our apartment, and she's trying to hide that she's a stress case about it for your sake. I know you think Andrew's the best thing that ever happened to Mom, but really, it's the other way around. So watch it, Minka." And Minka would just go, "Thaz nice."

As we walked down the street toward the avenue with all the shops, I attached my mittened hand to Minka's gloved hand. I told her, "Minka, you might possibly be a mad person. I don't know what we'll do when you finally leave because Meanie will be so spoiled by that time he will totally be impossible. That's your fault, you know, Minka."

Minka said, "Thaz nice."

I think there is some sanitation law or something about dogs not being allowed in coffee shops, but there must be some exception for fat cats on leashes, because no one said anything when Minka and I stomped in with Meanie. In fact, the owner said something to Minka in Polish and she laughed like a schoolgirl with a crush. Then she picked Meanie up into her arms and gave him a nose kiss. Whoa. Meanie barely lets me pet him. The owner showed us to a corner booth table at the window, and he put a dry towel on the seat for Meanie to perch on and look out the window, like that was their routine every day.

Minka handed the menu to me. I said, "Minka, Mom doesn't mind if I have a chocolate milk shake for breakfast."

Minka said, "Yez." Then she pointed to the overhead TV in the corner. "Regis!" she exclaimed, and clapped her hands.

For a smoking, complaining old person, Minka wasn't such bad company, to be honest. Minka didn't care if I played with my Game Boy at the table, which Mom never lets me do because she says it's rude. Minka laughed at the TV whenever the studio audience laughed, which put me in a happy-laughy mood. During the commercials, Minka talked in Polish to the Polish people at the other tables, who all seemed to know her and like her. She batted her eyelids a million times when the owner brought to our table a complimentary plate of *chrusciki,* which are these thin, crispy, sugar-dusted cookies that looked like angels' wings. I'd been to this coffee shop many times with Mom and Andrew before Minka came along, and first, I'd never seen these *chrusciki* things here before, and second, I'd never seen the old owner guy do anything but scowl at customers. When I said, "*Dziękuję,*" *thank you* in Polish, to the coffee shop man, Minka leaped up to give me a hug.

After the coffee shop, Minka took Meanie and me to Prospect Park. The snow had stopped falling, but the streets weren't all plowed yet and hadn't turned disgusting colors from cars, people, and animals, so it was truly like walking through a white winter paradise. People skied through the park and lots of kids toted sleds. Minka sat down on a bench, placed a dry towel on her lap, and lifted Meanie onto it. As she lit a cigarette, I dropped to the ground in front of her to make snow angels, which I decided to call *chrusciki* angels.

I wished I'd brought a sled when I saw Chrissy coming my way with two other girls from our school. "Hi," Chrissy said when she saw me on the ground. She didn't say hi to Minka, even though she knew perfectly well who Minka was. Chrissy says it's too hard trying to talk to someone who won't speak English, so why bother. "Can I come sled with you guys?" I asked.

Chrissy shook her head. "There's only room on the sled for us three. See ya later, Kate." She waved g'bye and the girls headed on their way. Chrissy is like that. One day you're her best friend and the next day she can't be bothered with you.

Minka blew smoke in Chrissy's direction and muttered, "*Jesteś glupia*," which I hope means Chrissy should possibly by the grace of God be knocked over by a falling tree branch. Minka isn't like my real grandma, who probably would have promised to bake chocolate chip cookies to make me feel better. Minka won't spoil a kid with presents and treats like a real grandma who wants to lock in your devotion. It's more like Minka will take her time to decide if she likes you and if you're worth her time, like Meanie. Maybe Minka doesn't hate all children.

When we got back home, we listened to a message on the answering machine from the English school asking if Minka was ever going to show up for her registered class. I'm sure Minka didn't understand the exact words, but she recognized the person's voice and understood the message. Her face turned guilty and she at least knew the English word *delete,* because her finger pushed that button before the answering machine voice finished speaking.

Minka toweled off Meanie's wet fur while I went to my room for some stuff. I returned to the kitchen and sat down at the table with Minka. I held up the brochure for the English school. Minka said, "*Jesteś szalona!*" which I know means "You're crazy!" because Minka has said that enough times to Mom that I've memorized the phrase and my Polish friend at school told me what it means. I looked at Minka. I thought, *She's not so bad, really. If even Meanie likes her, and the scowl-y coffee shop guy, she has to be an okay person. Maybe she shouldn't go back to Warsaw until she's really given Brooklyn a chance.*

I held up a Skipper doll and banged her against my chest. "Skipper, me," I told Minka. I held up a Barbie doll and pointed her toward Minka. "Barbie, you," I added. Then I placed Skipper's and Barbie's hands together and had them walk down the table, landing on the brochure for the English school. I said, "I could help you with English classes. We can start this afternoon by watching a movie together. I can explain to you what the actors are saying."

I placed my backpack on the table and took out a DVD. Chrissy isn't all bad — she does share her PG-13 movies that Mom doesn't let me watch. Minka might not speak English, but she sure perked up at the face on the cover of the movie. She said, "YEZ! Johnny Depp!"

I placed my index finger and thumb together and made the zip lip sign across my mouth. "First word today, Minka. SECRET! This movie will be our SECRET!" I zipped my fingers across my mouth again.

"Zee-creet," Minka repeated, also zipping her fingers across her mouth.

I got up from the table to head into the living room. I stopped at the fridge and pulled out the babka that Minka had made the day before. "Movie snack for us!" I said.

Another *look* from Minka, but this one was more

like she'd eaten a half-sour pickle: startled, but pleased. She pulled Meanie into her arms to bring him along for our movie. Minka must be a psychic, because I happen to know Meanie is a huge Johnny Depp fan.

"We can practice English now, Minka," I said. "Is Meanie your friend?"

"You is," Minka said, following me. "Katya-Kate."

DOLL
by Virginia Euwer Wolff

SOMEBODY SAID, "Let's everybody bring our dolls on Monday." I don't remember whose idea it was, our voices sounded so much alike. One of us first graders. One of the Janices or Bettys. Or Sandra, maybe. One doll. Our favorite, or the one our mothers would let us bring, one that had enough clothes not to freeze to death. Doll rules were very clear: Keep your doll warm, talk nice to it, give it a place to sleep, and make up conversation for it to have. Some girls didn't bother feeding their dolls; some did. It didn't matter in the long run. The dolls all looked the same, basically. Chubby and pink and kind of used-looking, from having their clothes taken off and put on, having their faces washed and their hair played with, or being fed pieces of cake or banana.

We would all bring our dolls on Monday.

One of the teacher favorites — it's hard to remember which one of us it was after all these years — asked the teacher in a primpy voice, "It's all right for us to bring our dolls on Monday, isn't it?" And of course it was.

It must have been a Wednesday. When we went outside for recess the girls were all talking about which dolls they would bring to school on Monday, and somehow I got next to Jeanie, waiting in line to go down the slide.

Jeanie wasn't somebody anyone would get next to on purpose, because she smelled like urine and she had pointy hair and bruises on her spindly arms and legs, and many of the bruises had little dark things in them, sores or something. Her bruises were slow to heal; you could watch the same one at story circle time for weeks. And her face was always gazing somewhere sideways from where everyone else was focusing.

But we were good children who mostly went to Sunday School, and nobody ever actually ran away from Jeanie. You might roll your eyes and wrinkle up your nose if you had to get next to her in any of the lines we had to form: lunch line, hand-washing line, fire drill line, vaccination line for the county health nurse who came with needles for our betterment. Jeanie was always looking somewhat away from you, so she may never have noticed those rolled eyes.

While we waited in the slide line, I looked Jeanie as

straight in the face as she would allow, and I asked her, "You gonna bring a doll on Monday?"

She looked at my shoulder and said, in her soft, flat voice, "I don't have no doll."

The sun shone on the maple trees at the edge of the playground, giving the leaves a friendly look. The trees were a kindly presence, in the same way that the minister and the janitor and the phys ed teacher and the principal's dog all were. Our town tolerated our childhoods and wished us well as we grew, and nobody doubted any of it.

I don't have no doll.

I don't have no doll.

I had never heard anyone say such a thing, although I knew that the starving Armenian children surely didn't have dolls, and the little English children had mostly lost their dolls in the Blitz. We weren't entirely ignorant of the war going on, but nobody had told us very much, either.

We knew only what we knew, and if we hadn't heard someone say a thing before, there had to be a first time.

I don't have no doll.

What went through my head didn't require an explanation, a reason, an argument, anything. I just made a decision, simple enough.

That afternoon, when the school bus had dropped

us off at the foot of the road and we'd walked up the hill, picking dandelions and watching squirrels in the trees, I told my mother, "We're gonna bring our dolls to school on Monday, but Jeanie doesn't have one. So let's buy her a doll."

My mother was the church organist and a farmer and a gentle person. She fetched the pitcher of milk and the graham crackers and plates and glasses, and we sat at the kitchen table having our snack. "Do you think that's what she wants you to do?" she asked.

I hadn't thought to wonder. "Why would she not? Who wouldn't want a doll? Come on, please?"

We went to the general store and looked at the dolls. They had three kinds of babies, and we chose the middle-price one. She had everything she needed: a dress, shoes, socks, a blanket. She didn't come with a bottle or a bonnet, but those weren't essential things. We asked the clerk to put her in a doll box. We took her home and wrapped the box, but not fancy. Just a hair ribbon, ironed and tied in a bow. I took it to school on Friday morning, inside a grocery bag. I met Jeanie beside our cubbies and gave her the box. "This is for you," I said. I wasn't sure how to have a conversation with Jeanie, with her face turned to the side and her bruises. She untied the hair ribbon, opened the box, and looked at the doll. "That's real nice," she said solemnly.

She stroked the doll's hair and said again, "That's real nice."

Maybe nobody saw; certainly nobody asked.

My mother wouldn't let me take any of my three Madame Alexander dolls to school. (We could not help having a rich uncle who gave me the dolls. That was not our fault.) So Sonja Henie, Margaret O'Brien, and Scarlett O'Hara stayed at home crowded together on the bench where they lived most of the time, their big, alluring eyes staring at chairs. I felt bad having to choose a doll from among the babies in my bedroom. Each one had a different kind of shoes, and each one had something amiss because I couldn't let them alone. One had cocoa spilled on her dress; one had hair that wouldn't right itself; one's blanket had disappeared behind the toy chest and had not come back.

I chose Peggy with the broken-off foot. She had slept on my bed with me, and in my sleep I had knocked her onto the floor and she'd lost half her foot. I found her bonnet, put booties on her, and wrapped her in a blanket I borrowed from Gloria. I told Gloria and the other dolls they would all get their turns, but it was right for Peggy to be the first one to get to go to school, because of her foot.

On Monday we girls all had dolls, and the boys seemed not to notice. When some of them stopped ignoring us long enough to tease us they got ignored right back, so they stopped. A few of us fed our dolls from our lunches. We had rice pudding for dessert from the school kitchen and somebody began reciting:

> *"What is the matter with Mary Jane?*
> *She's perfectly well and she hasn't a pain,*
> *And it's LOVELY rice pudding for dinner*
> *aGAYN!"*

Not everybody knew that poem, but we taught it to them, and then we all chanted it to our dolls.

Jeanie said some of it along with us, although she didn't make her voice go loud. She had the newest doll of anybody. There was some whispering about it, but not much.

Two of the girls had to put their dolls away in their cubbies during Numbers Time because they couldn't keep their eyes on the blackboard with dolls in their laps. Other than that, the day was just a day. A day of dolls at school, of girls comparing their children, comforting and coddling their children, hoisting and carrying them, trading clothes for them, shushing them, and going on with getting an education.

Jeanie held her new doll in basic nursing position all day long, weighting the paper and printing her letters with the other hand. She didn't ask anyone else to watch her doll while she went to the bathroom. She didn't chatter about dolls, but we didn't expect her to. Jeanie didn't ever talk much.

The important thing, as far as I was concerned, was that Jeanie had a doll that day. That she wasn't left out. Good heavens, with her bruises and her wandering look and her stink and her silence, she was already left out enough.

So I was satisfied. Jeanie had a doll and she seemed to like it.

Nothing really changed.

Once in a while in the next few years, as I was turning over to go to sleep in my bedroom full of dolls, I thought about what my mother had said: "Do you think that's what she wants you to do?"

When we were in fourth grade I got a copy of *Understood Betsy* for Christmas. In the story, Betsy and her friends get together in a burst of charity and sew new clothing for the poor little dirty orphan boy in their one-room school. Their sin is that they gloat over their own generosity.

Soul-searching was still such a new thing to me that I didn't know how to do it. I began by asking myself, "Did I gloat about giving Jeanie the doll that time? It wasn't even my own money that bought it. Did I gloat?"

For the life of me, I couldn't remember. It was only three years back that I had put the box in Jeanie's hands and she had stroked the doll's hair and murmured, "That's real nice." But I couldn't remember if I had gloated or not.

As we grew older and went to junior high, I had music lessons and trips, and Jeanie mostly had more of what she had always had. Still a few bruises, the remote glance, the muted, serious voice. She no longer smelled like urine, but as puberty came along the phys ed teacher took her aside and gave her some deodorant. It was what teachers did: They tried to make up for things that were missing or not understood.

Some people said her father had gone away, just left. Around their house, on the side road behind the general store, were dogs and dog bones and dog chains and one gnawed sofa.

Social lines were less elastic than when we had been first graders, and as we grew Jeanie and I sat in different groups at assemblies, at different tables in the lunchroom. Jeanie had people to walk with and sit with, other quiet, new, faded kids in rummage-sale clothing. Her voice was still soft and noncommittal, but she voted in school elections and gave halting reports in social studies, and she moved inward from the fringes of the class photos.

And then we went to high school, where Jeanie turned out to be the best volleyball setter in the school's history. People talked about it in the lunchroom; the coach put an arm around her in the hallway. The PTA bought her a regulation volleyball uniform and shoes. Grown-ups from our town and the next town over came to see the games as we had never known them to do.

One day when we were fifteen, I had a dentist appointment and got to school late, without a note from the dentist or from my mother. A simple case of absentmindedness. The principal's secretary was not going to let me go to band class, and I hated to miss band. Jeanie came by the office to get an aspirin for a headache, saw me with my clarinet case, and heard what was going on. She looked sideways at the secretary and said in her low, even voice, "Let her go to band — what's the matter with you?"

Stacks of the school newspaper lay on the office

counter, with Jeanie in a photograph on the front page, wearing her team shirt and shorts, ready to set the ball, her pointy hair back in a ponytail, her muscular legs and arms flexed in taut symmetry, and not a bruise in sight.

The secretary's hand lifted just a bit off the counter, its pencil rising up and then sinking back down. Her jaw moved slightly. She wrote me a pass to band class, frowned at me for being forgetful, and Jeanie and I walked out of the office together and down the hall before separating to go in different directions. "Thanks, Jeanie," I said. "That was a brave thing to do."

"Forget it — it was nothing," Jeanie said soberly, and smiled sideways at me. Two of her teeth were already rotting, visible when she smiled.

In the chaos of repeating over and over how much we hated high school and couldn't wait to get out of there, of some of us applying to college and others moving away or getting married or joining the air force — and then in the hurry of graduating and driving our parents' cars and some of the rougher boys having accidents and ending up crippled and hanging around the Texaco station looking bitter with constricted rage — in that hectic time of trying to turn into adults, we all veered in our different directions.

Decades have gone by. Wars and peaces and losses and change. I have hunted for the right questions to ask. Is human integrity the most important thing? Whom can we trust and can we be trusted? What is love? When we reflect on our lives, what do we find?

Jeanie's face appears in my dreams from time to time. In one dream we're all trying to recite together, "And it's LOVELY rice pudding for dinner aGAYN!" But we never chant it in unison; there are syllables sticking out everywhere.

And sometimes she's at the net, setting the volleyball. Wordless, tense, dignified, staring at the ball head-on, heroic.

Do I ever see Jeanie when I visit our hometown? Would I recognize her, or she, me? I drive past the elementary school and its maple trees, shining in the sun or dripping with rain. They look like the same maple trees our parents stood under and cried when they came to school to pick us up on the day President Roosevelt died.

I drive past the high school and remember how the gym shook with the screams of volleyball fans as Jeanie and the team took our school to the only three consecutive district victories it ever won. Now the students attend a large, consolidated high school eighteen miles away, and our old school has craft and exercise classes and Veterans of Foreign Wars meetings.

I buy a few things at the general store, which burned down and was rebuilt after the Vietnam War. I drive past the church, which now has a wheelchair-accessible ramp leading to a side door. The pine trees next to the church are gone; they were planted by my grandparents and three other first families who settled in the town a century ago, and they grew into a bushy grove, but the church congregation voted to remove them and put in a parking lot when Richard Nixon was president.

Do I pass Jeanie when I drive through the town? What does she look like?

Did she marry a man who beat her and then drank himself to death? It happened to some. Not many, but some. Did she go away? What did she do with her strong body?

Did she end up liking the doll? Did she give it a name, take its clothes off, try to feed it, talk nice to it and make up its replies? What did she ask her doll?

My mother's question: "Do you think that's what she wants you to do?" When I was six years old, I didn't even think it was worth my attention.

Did Jeanie keep the doll? Did someone take it away

from her? Who? Why? Did she end up throwing it away? Did she save it, let it become an antique, and give it to a granddaughter?

Did I gloat? And did she ever forgive me for that?

Or does she hate me?

ABOUT THE AUTHORS

MEG CABOT is the #1 *New York Times* bestselling author of the Princess Diaries series, as well as many other bestselling books for teen readers, including *All-American Girl, Teen Idol,* and the Mediator and 1-800-Where-R-U series. Meg currently divides her time between Key West, Florida, and New York City with her husband and one-eyed cat, Henrietta.

RACHEL COHN grew up in Silver Spring, Maryland. In elementary school, her best friends were Lena, Terri, Marianne, and Nanette. At lunch during the 6th grade, Nanette regularly traded her Skippy peanut butter and jelly on white bread sandwiches and Little Debbie Snack Cakes for Rachel's all-natural slush peanut butter and jelly on wheat bread sandwiches and granola bar desserts. Rachel realizes this was an unfair trade and would like to thank Nanette for her magnanimous generosity. Rachel now lives in New York City, and her best friends are Stephanie, Daina, Maura, and Elizabeth.

TANUJA DESAI HIDIER'S first novel, *Born Confused,* was an ALA Top Ten Best Book for Teens. Tanuja has also worked as a filmmaker and is currently adapting *Born Confused* into a screenplay. She is the lead singer/songwriter in both the London-based band San Transisto and the NYC rock duo T&A. *When We Were Twins*, their CD of original rock/pop/electro-folk songs based on *Born Confused*, is now available worldwide. Please visit www.ABCreativeD.com for more info on all.

JENNIFER L. HOLM is the author of the Newbery Honor–winning *Our Only May Amelia*, as well as the *Boston Jane* trilogy, and the young adult novel *The Creek*. She is currently working on a graphic novel series with one of her best friends, her brother Matt.

PATRICK JENNINGS has moved 31 times in 38 years. His latest book is called *Out Standing in My Field*. He writes, "My best friend Troy crashed one day when a bunch of us guys were riding bikes around a dirt track we'd worn into a vacant lot. When he got up, we all gasped: One of his arms looked as if it had two elbows. I walked Troy and both our bikes to his house. He cried like a baby the whole way. I remember wishing it were my arm that got busted. Being his best friend, I was first to sign his cast."

DAVID LEVITHAN is the founding editor of the PUSH imprint at Scholastic, and edits many other wonderful authors. He is also the author of *Boy Meets Boy*, *The Realm of Possibility*, and *Are We There Yet?* He grew up in New Jersey and still lives there.

ANN M. MARTIN is the author of *Here Today*; *A Corner of the Universe*, winner of a 2003 Newbery Honor; and *Belle Teal*. She feels very lucky to have been able to collaborate on other titles with some of her best friends—with the late Paula Danziger on *P.S. Longer Letter Later* and *Snail Mail No More*, and with Laura Godwin and Brian Selznick on *The Doll People* and *The Meanest Doll in the World*. She lives in upstate New York with three cats and her dog Sadie—who sparked the idea for "Squirrel."

PATRICIA McCORMICK grew up in Pennsylvania and currently lives in New York, where she has coffee every Friday with her two best friends. There is no Elizabeth Larue in her past, but this story was inspired by a real-life incident that exposed the dark underside of friendship. She is the author of *Cut* and *My Brother's Keeper*.

PAM MUÑOZ RYAN has written many books for young people, including the novels *Riding Freedom*, *Esperanza Rising*, and *Becoming Naomi León*. She says, "I would have liked to have been friends with some of the heroines in my books. If I had known them, maybe I could have absorbed their qualities I so admire. Maybe I could have been as courageous as Charlotte in *Riding Freedom*, as adventurous as Amelia Earhart and Eleanor Roosevelt in *Amelia and Eleanor Go for a Ride*, or as determined as Marian Anderson in *When Marian Sang*. I'm sure those worthy women would have changed my life."

BRIAN SELZNICK is the Caldecott Honor–winning illustrator of *The Dinosaurs of Waterhouse Hawkins*, as well as other books including *The Houdini Box*, *When Marian Sang*, and *Walt*. He lives in Brooklyn, New York.

VIRGINIA EUWER WOLFF has been thinking about friendship since World War II. She is the author of five novels for young readers: *Probably Still Nick Swansen*, *Make Lemonade*, *The Mozart Season*, *Bat 6*, and *True Believer*.

 **The Lisa Libraries**

In 1990, the Lisa Libraries was established by author Ann M. Martin and friends to honor and memorialize children's book editor Lisa Novak. In Lisa's name, new books are collected from authors, editors, publishers, and other supporters, and sorted into small libraries to be donated to organizations serving needy children.

Libraries have been established in day-care centers, at after-school programs, and in prison visiting areas for children of incarcerated parents. The Lisa Libraries also provides books to children who may never have owned a book before.

For more information about the Lisa Libraries, please visit: www.lisalibraries.org.